Mrs. Hungerford

April's Lady

Vol. III

Mrs. Hungerford

April's Lady
Vol. III

ISBN/EAN: 9783337053000

Printed in Europe, USA, Canada, Australia, Japan

Cover: Foto ©Andreas Hilbeck / pixelio.de

More available books at **www.hansebooks.com**

A Novel.

BY

MRS. HUNGERFORD,

AUTHOR OF

"MOLLY BAWN," "PHYLLIS," "A LIFE'S REMORSE,"
"HER LAST THROW," ETC., ETC.

IN THREE VOLUMES.

VOL. III.

LONDON:

F. V. WHITE & CO.,
31, SOUTHAMPTON STREET, STRAND, W.C.
1891.

CONTENTS.

APRIL'S LADY.

APRIL'S LADY.

CHAPTER I.

"'Tis said the rose is Love's own flower,
  Its blush so bright—its thorns so many."

THERE is no mistake in the joy with which Felix parts from his companions after luncheon. He breathes afresh as he sees them tearing up the staircase to get ready for their afternoon walk, Nurse puffing and panting behind them.

The drawing-room seems a bower of repose after the turmoil of the late feast, and, besides, it cannot be long now before she—they—return. That is if they—*she*—return at all! He has, indeed, ample time given him to imagine this last horrible possibility as not only a probability, but a certainty, before the sound of coming footsteps up the stairs and the *frou-frou* of pretty frocks tells him his doubts were harmless. Involuntarily he rises from his chair, and straightens himself out of the rather forlorn position into which he has fallen, and fixes his eyes immovably upon the door. Are there *two* of them?

That is beyond doubt. It is only mad people who chatter to themselves, and certainly Mrs. Monkton is not mad.

Barbara has indeed raised her voice a little more than ordinary, and has addressed Joyce by her name on her hurried way up the staircase and across the cushioned recess outside the door. Now she throws open the door and enters, radiant, if a little nervous.

"Here we are," she says, very pleasantly, and with all the put-on manner of one who has made up her mind to be extremely joyous under distinct difficulties. "You are still here, then, and alone. They didn't murder you. Joyce and I had our misgivings all along. Ah, I forgot, you haven't seen Joyce until now."

"How d'ye do?" says Miss Kavanagh, holding out her hand to him, with a calm as perfect as her smile.

"I *do* hope they were good," goes on Mrs. Monkton, her nervousness rather increasing. "You know I have always said they were the best children in the world."

"Ah! said, *said*," repeats Mrs. Monkton, who now seems grateful for the chance of saying anything. What is the meaning of Joyce's sudden amiability—and *is* it amiability, or——

"It is true one can say almost anything," says Joyce, quite pleasantly. She nods her head prettily at Dysart. "There is no law to prevent them. Barbara thinks you are not sincere. She is not fair to you. You always *do* mean what you say, don't you?"

But for the smile that accompanies these words, Dysart would have felt his doom sealed. But could she mean a stab so cruel, so direct, and still look kind?

"Oh! he *is* always sincere," says Barbara, quickly, "only people say things about one's children, you know, that——." She stops.

"They are the dearest children. You are a bad mother; you wrong them," says Joyce, laughing lightly, plainly at the idea of Barbara's affection for her children being impugned. "She told me," turning her lovely eyes full on Dysart, with no special expression in them, whatever, "that I should find only your remains after spending an hour with them." Her smile is brilliant.

"She was wrong, you see. I am still here," says Felix, hardly knowing what he says, in his desire to read her face, which is strictly impassive.

"Yes, still here," says Miss Kavanagh, smiling, always, and apparently meaning nothing at all; yet to Felix, watching her, there seems to be something treacherous in her manner.

"*Still here?*" Had she hoped he would be gone? Was that the cause of her delay?

Had she purposely put off coming home to give him time to grow tired and go away? And yet she is looking at him with a smile!

"I am afraid you had a bad luncheon and a bad time generally," says Mrs. Monkton quickly, who seems hurried in every way. "But we came home as soon as ever we could. Didn't we, Joyce?" Her appeal to her sister is suggestive of fear as to the answer, but she need not have been nervous about that.

"We *flew!*" declares Miss Kavanagh with delightful zeal. "We thought we should never get here soon enough. Didn't we, Barbara?" There is the very barest, faintest imitation of her sister's voice in this last question; a subtle touch of mockery, so slight, so evanescent as to leave one doubtful as to its ever having existed.

"Yes, yes, indeed," says Barbara colouring.

"We flew so fast indeed that I am sure

you are thoroughly fatigued," says Miss Kavanagh, addressing her. " Why don't you run away now, and take off your bonnet and lie down for an hour or so ? "

"But," begins Barbara, and then stops short. What does it all mean ? this new departure of her sister's puzzles her. To so deliberately ask for a *tête-à-tête* with Felix ! To what end ?   The girl's manner, so bright, filled with such a glittering geniality—so unlike the usual listlessness that has characterized it for so long—both confuses and alarms her. Why is she so amiable now ? There had been a little difficulty about getting her back at all, quite enough to make Mrs. Monkton shiver for Dysart's reception by her, and here, now, half-an-hour later, she is beaming upon him and being more than ordinarily civil. What is she going to do ?

" Oh ! no ' buts,' " says Joyce gaily. " You know you said your head was aching, and Mr. Dysart will excuse you.   He will not be so badly off even without you. He will have *me!*" She turns a full glance on Felix as she says this, and looks at him with lustrous eyes and white teeth showing through her parted lips. The *soupçon* of mockery in her whole air, of which all through he has been faintly but uncomfortably aware, has deepened. "I shall take care he is not dull."

"But," says Barbara again rather helplessly.

"No, no. You *must* rest yourself. Remember we are going to that 'at home' at the Thesigers' to-night, and I would not miss it for anything. Don't dwell with such sad looks on Mr. Dysart, I have promised to look after him. You will *let* me take care of you for a little while, Mr. Dysart, will you not?" turning another brilliant smile upon Felix who responds to it very gravely.

He is regarding her with a searching air. How is it with her? Some old words recur to him.

" There is treachery, O Ahaziah ! "

Why does she look at him like that ?   He
mistrusts her present attitude.   Even that
aggressive mood of hers at the Doré Gallery
on that last day when they met, was pre-
ferable to this agreeable but detestable indifference.

" It is always a pleasure to be with you,"
says he steadily, perhaps a little doggedly.

" There ! you see ! " says Joyce with a
pretty little nod at her sister.

" Well, I shall take half-an-hour's rest,"
says Mrs. Monkton reluctantly, who is, in
truth, feeling as fresh as a daisy, but who is
afraid to stay.   " But I shall be back for tea."
She gives a little kindly glance to Felix, and
with a heart filled with forebodings leaves the
room.

" What a glorious day it has been ! "
says Joyce, continuing the conversation with
Dysart in that new manner of hers, quite as
if Barbara's going was a matter of small importance, and the fact that she has left them,

for the first time for all these months, alone together, of less importance still.

She is standing on the hearthrug, and is slowly taking the pins out of her bonnet. She seems utterly unconcerned. He might be the veriest stranger, or else the oldest, the most uninteresting friend in the world.

She has taken out all the pins now, and has thrown her bonnet on to the lounge nearest to her, and is standing before the glass in the overmantel patting and pushing into order the soft locks that lie upon her forehead.

CHAPTER II.

" Ah, were she pitiful as she is fair."

" Life's a varied, bright illusion,
    Joy and sorrow—light and shade."

"It was almost warm," says she turning round to him. She seems to be talking all the time, so vivid is her face, so intense her vitality. "I was so glad to see the Brabazons again. *You* know them, don't you? Kit looked perfect. So lovely, so good in every way—voice, face, manner. I felt I envied her. It would be delightful to feel that everyone *must* be admiring one, as she does." She glances at him and he leans a little towards her. "No, no, not a compliment, *please*. I know I am as much behind Kit as the moon is behind the sun."

"I wasn't going to pay you a compliment," says he slowly.

" No ? " she laughs. It was unlike her to have made that remark, and just as unlike her to have taken his rather discourteous reply so good-naturedly.

" It was a charming visit," she goes on, not in haste, but idly as it were, and as if words are easy to her. " I quite enjoyed it. Barbara didn't. I think she wanted to get home—she is always thinking of the babies—or——. Well, *I* did. I am not ungrateful. I take the goods the Gods provide, and find honest pleasure in them. I do not think, indeed, I laughed so much for quite a century as to-day with Kit."

" She is sympathetic," says Felix, with the smallest thought of the person in question in his mind.

" More than that, surely. Though *that* is a hymn of praise in itself. After all it is a relief to meet Irish people when one has spent a week or two in stolid England. You agree with me ? "

" I am English," returns he.

" Oh !   Of *course !* How rude of me !   I
didn't mean it however.   I had entirely forgotten :—our acquaintance having been con-
fined entirely to Irish soil until this luckless
moment !   You *do* forgive me ? "

She is leaning a little forward, and looking
at him with a careless expression.

" No," returns he briefly.

" Well, you should," says she, taking no
notice of his cold rejoinder, and treating it
indeed as if it is of no moment.   If there was
a deeper meaning in his refusal to grant her
absolution she declines to acknowledge it.
" Still, even that *bêtise* of mine need not
prevent you from seeing some truth in my
argument.   We *have* our charms, we Irish,
eh ? "

" *Your* charm ? "

" Well, mine, if you like, as a type, and "
—recklessly, and with a shrug of her shoulders—" if you wish to be personal."

She has gone a little too far.

" I think I have acknowledged that," says

he coldly. He rises abruptly, and goes over to where she is standing on the hearth-rug—shading her face from the fire, with a huge Japanese fan. " Have I ever denied your charm ? " His tone has been growing in intensity, and now becomes stern. " Why do you talk to me like this ? What is the meaning of it all—your altered manner—everything ? Why did you grant me this interview ? "

" Perhaps because "—still with that radiant smile, bright and cold as early frost—" like that little soapy boy, I thought you would ' not be happy till you got it.' "

She laughs lightly. The laugh is the outcome of the smile, and its close imitation. It is perfectly successful, but on the surface only. There is no heart in it.

" You think I arranged it ? "

" Oh, no ; how could I ? You have just said I arranged it." She shuts up her fan with a little click. " You want to say some-thing, don't you ? " says she, " well, say it ! "

"You give me permission, then?" asks he, gravely, despair knocking at his heart.

"Why not—would I have you unhappy always?" Her tone is jesting throughout.

"You think"—taking the hand that holds the fan, and restraining its motion for a moment, "that if I do speak I shall be happier?"

"Ah! that is beyond me," says she. "And yet—yes; to get a thing over is to get rid of fatigue. I have argued it all out for myself, and have come to the conclusion——"

"For *yourself!*"

"Well, for you too"—a little impatiently. "After all, it is you who want to speak. Silence, to me, is golden. But it occurred to me in the silent watches of the night," with another—now rather forced—little laugh, "that if you once said to me all you had to say, you would be contented, and go away, and not trouble me any more."

"I can do that now, without saying anything," says he slowly. He has dropped her hand ; he is evidently deeply wounded.

"Can you ?"

Her eyes are resting relentlessly on his. Is there magic in them ? . . . Her mouth has taken a strange expression.

"I might have known how it would be," says Dysart, throwing up his head. "You will not forgive ! It was but a moment— a few words, idle, hardly considered, and——"

"Oh, yes, *considered !* " says she slowly.

"They were unmeant ! " persists he fiercely. "I defy you to think otherwise. One great mistake—a second's madness—and you have ordained that it shall wreck my whole life ! *You !*—That evening in the library at the Court. I had not thought of——"

"Ah ! " she interrupts him, even more by her gesture—which betrays the first touch of passion she has shown—than by her voice, that is still mocking. "I *knew* you would have to say it ! "

"You know me, indeed ! " says he, with

an enforced calmness that leaves him very white. "My whole heart and soul lie bare to you, to ruin as you will. It is the merest waste of time, I know; but still, I have felt all along that I *must* tell you again that I love you, though I fully understand I shall receive nothing in return but scorn and contempt. Still, to be able even to say it is a relief to me."

"And what is it to me?" asks the girl, as pale now as he is; "is it a relief—a comfort to *me* to have to listen to you?"

She clenches her hands involuntarily. The fan falls with a little crash to the ground.

"No." He is silent a moment. "No—it is unfair—unjust! You shall not be made uncomfortable again. . . . It is the last time. . . . I shall not trouble you again in this way. I don't say we shall never meet again. You"— pausing and looking at her—"you do not desire *that?*"

"Oh, no," coldly, politely.

"If you do, say so at once," with a rather peremptory ring in his tone.

"I should," calmly.

"I am glad of that. As my cousin is a great friend of mine, and as I shall get a fortnight's leave soon, I shall probably run over to Ireland, and spend it with her. After all"—bitterly—"why should I suppose it would be disagreeable to you?"

"It was quite a natural idea," says she immovably.

"However," says he steadily, "you need not be afraid that, even if we do meet, I shall ever annoy you in this way again——"

"Oh, I am never afraid," says she, with that terrible smile that seems to freeze him.

"Well, good-bye," holding out his hand. He is quite as composed as she is now, and is even able to return her smile in kind.

"So soon? But Barbara will be down to tea in a few minutes. You will surely wait for her?"

"I think not."

"But really *do!* I am going to see after the children, and give them some chocolate I bought for them."

"It will probably make them ill," says he, smiling still. "No, thank you. I must go now, indeed. You will make my excuses to Mrs. Monkton, please. Good-bye."

"Good-bye," says she, laying her hand in his for a second. She has grown suddenly very cold, shivering, it seems almost as if an icy blast from some open portal has been blown in upon her. He is still looking at her. There is something wild—strange —in his expression.

"You cannot realize it, but I can," says he, unsteadily. "It is good-bye for ever so far as life for *me* is concerned!"

He has turned away from her. He is gone. The sharp closing of the door wakens her to the fact that she is alone. Mechanically, quite calmly, she looks round the empty room. There is a little Persian chair-cover over there all awry. She re-arranges it with a critical eye to its proper appearance, and afterwards pushes a small chair into its place. She pats a cushion or two, and finally taking up her bonnet and the pins she had laid upon the chimney-piece, goes up to her own room.

Once there——

With a rush the whole thing comes back to her. The entire meaning of it—what she has done. That word—*for ever*. The bonnet has fallen from her fingers. Sinking upon her knees beside the bed, she buries her face out of sight. Presently her slender frame is torn by those cruel, yet merciful sobs !

*   *   *   *   .   *

CHAPTER III.

"The sense of death is most in apprehension."

"Thus grief still treads upon the heels of pleasure."

IT is destined to be a day of grief! Monkton,
who had been out all the morning, having
gone to see the old people, a usual habit
of his, had not returned to dinner—a very
unusual habit with him. It had occurred,
however, once or twice, that he had stayed
to dine with them on such occasions, as when
Sir George had had a troublesome letter from
his elder son, and had looked to the younger
to give him some comfort—some of his time,
to help him to bear it, by talking it all over.
Barbara, therefore, whilst dressing for Mrs.
Thesiger's " At Home," had scarcely felt
anxiety, and, indeed, it is only now when
she has come down to the drawing-room to
find Joyce awaiting her, also in gala garb,

so far as a gown goes, that a suspicion of coming trouble takes possession of her.

"He is late, isn't he?" she says, looking at Joyce with something nervous in her expression. "What can have kept him? I know he wanted to meet the General, and now——What *can* it be?"

"His mother, probably," says Joyce indifferently. "From your description of her, I should say she must be a most thoroughly uncomfortable old person."

"Yes. Not pleasant, certainly. A little of her, as George Ingram used to say, goes a long way. But still——And these Thesiger people are friends of his, and——"

"You are working yourself up into a thorough belief in the sensational street accident," says Joyce, who has seated herself well out of the glare of the chandelier. "You want to be tragic. It is a mistake, believe me."

Something in the bitterness of the girl's tone strikes on her sister's ear. Joyce had not come down to dinner, had pleaded a headache as an excuse for her non-appearance, and Mrs. Monkton and Tommy (she could not bear to dine alone) had devoured that meal *à deux*. Tommy certainly had been anything but dull company.

"Has anything happened, Joyce?" asks her sister quickly. She has had her suspicions of course, but they were of the vaguest order.

Joyce laughs.

"I *told* you your nerves were out of order," says she. "What should happen? Are you still dwelling on the running over business? I assure you, you wrong Freddy. He can take care of himself at a crossing as well as another man, and better. Even a hansom, I am convinced, could do no harm to Freddy."

"I wasn't thinking of him," says Barbara, a little reproachfully, perhaps. "I——"

"No. Then you ought to be ashamed of yourself? Here he *is*," cries she suddenly, springing to her feet, as the sound of Monkton's footsteps ascending the stairs can be now distinctly heard. " I hope you will explain yourself to *him!*" She laughs again and disappears through the doorway that leads to the second hall outside, as Monkton enters.

" How late you are, Freddy," says his wife, the reproach in her voice heightened because of the anxiety she has been enduring. " I thought you would never——What is it ? What has happened ? *Freddy !* there is bad news."

" Yes, very bad," says Monkton, sinking into a chair.

" Your brother——" breathlessly. Of late, she has always known that trouble is to be expected from him.

" He is dead," says Monkton in a low tone.

Barbara, flinging her opera cloak aside, comes quickly to him. She leans over him and slips her arms round his neck.

" *Dead !*" says she in an awestruck tone.

" Yes. Killed himself ! Shot himself !

The telegram came this morning when I was with them. I could not come home sooner; it was impossible to leave them."

"Oh! Freddy, I am sorry you left them even now; a line to me would have done. Oh, what a horrible thing, and to die like *that*."

"Yes." He presses one of her hands, and then rising, begins to move hurriedly up and down the room. "It was misfortune on misfortune," he says presently. "When I went over there this morning, they had just received a letter from him filled with——"

"From *him!*"

"Yes. That is what seemed to make it so much worse later on. Life in the morning, death in the afternoon!" His voice grows choked. "And *such* a letter as it was, filled with nothing but a most scandalous account of his—Oh!"——he breaks off suddenly as if shocked. "Oh, he is *dead*, poor fellow."

"Don't take it like that," says Barbara, following him and clinging to him. "You *know* you could not be unkind. There were debts then ? "

" Debts ! It is difficult to explain just now, my head is aching so, and those poor old people ! Well, it means ruin for them, Barbara. Of course his debts must be paid ; his honour kept intact, for the sake of the old name, but——They will let *all* the houses, the two in town, this one, and their own, and——and the old place down in Warwickshire, the *home*, all must go out of their hands."

" Oh, Freddy, surely—surely there must be some way——"

" Not one. I spoke about breaking the entail. You know I—his death, poor fellow. I——"

" Yes, yes, dear."

" But they wouldn't hear of it. My mother was very angry, even in her grief, when I proposed it. They hope that, by strict retrenchment, the property will right itself again ; and they spoke about Tommy. They said it would be unjust to him——"

" And to you," quickly. She would not have him ignored any longer.

" Oh, as for me, I'm not a boy, you know. Tommy is safe to inherit as life goes."

" Well, so are you," says she, with a sharp pang at her heart.

" Yes, of course. I am only making out a case. I think it was kind of them to remember Tommy's claim in the very midst of their own great grief."

" It was indeed," says she remorsefully. " Oh, it *was*. But if they give up everything, where will they go ? "

" They talk of taking a cottage—a small house somewhere. They want to give up everything to pay his infamous—— *There!*" sharply, " I am forgetting again ! But to see them, makes one forget everything else." He begins his walk up and down the room again, as if inaction is impossible to him. " My mother, who has been accustomed to a certain luxury all her life, to be now, at the very close of it, condemned to—— It

would break your heart to see her. And she
will let nothing be said of him."

" Oh, *no*."

" Still, there should be justice. I can't
help feeling that. *Her* blameless life, and
his——and *she* is the one to suffer."

" It is so often so," says his wife in a low
tone. " It is an old story, dearest, but I know
that when the old stories come home to us
individually they always sound so terribly
new. But what do they mean by a small
house ?" asks she presently in a distressed tone.

" Well, I suppose a small house," says he
with just a passing gleam of his old jesting
manner. " You know my mother cannot
bear the country, so I think the cottage
idea will fall through."

" Freddy," says his wife suddenly. " She
can't go into a small house, a *London* small
house. It is out of the question. Could
they not come and live with us ? "

She is suggesting a martyrdom for herself,
yet she does it unflinchingly.

"What! My aunt and all?" asks he, regarding her earnestly.

"Oh, of course, of course, poor old thing," says she, unable this time, however, to hide the quaver that desolates her voice.

"*No*," says her husband with a suspicion of vehemence. He takes her suddenly in his arms and kisses her. "Because two or three people are unhappy is no reason why a fourth should be made so, and I won't have your life spoiled, so far as *I* can prevent it. I suppose you have guessed that I must go over to Nice—where *he* is—my father could not possibly go alone in his present state."

"When must you go?"

"To-morrow. As for you——"

"If we could go home," says she uncertainly.

"That is what I would suggest, but how will you manage without me? The children are so troublesome when taken out of their usual beat, and their Nurse—I often wonder which would require the most looking after, they, or she? It occurred to me to ask Dysart to see you across."

"He is so kind, such a friend," says Mrs. Monkton. "But——"

She might have said more, but at this instant Joyce appears in the doorway.

"We shall be late," cries she, "and Freddy not even dressed, why——. Oh, has anything *really* happened?"

"Yes, yes," says Barbara hurriedly—a few words explain all. "We must go home to-morrow, you see; and Freddy thinks that Felix would look after us until we reached Kingstown or North Wall."

"Felix—Mr. Dysart?" The girl's face had grown pale during the recital of the suicide, but now she looks ghastly. "Why should he come?" cries she in a ringing tone that has actual fear in it. "Do you suppose that we two cannot manage the children between us? Oh, nonsense, Barbara; why Tommy is as sensible as he can

be, and if Nurse *does* prove incapable, and
a prey to sea-sickness, well—I can take
baby, and you can look after Mabel. It
will be all right! We are not going to
America really. Freddy, *please* say you will
not trouble Mr. Dysart about this matter."

"Yes. I really think we shall not require him," says Barbara. Something in
the glittering brightness of her sister's eye
warns her to give in at once, and indeed she
had been unconsciously a little half-hearted
about having Felix or any stranger as a
travelling companion. "There, run away,
Joyce, and go to your bed, darling, you
look very tired. I must still arrange some
few things with Freddy."

"What is the matter with her?" asks
Monkton, when Joyce has gone away. "She
looks as if she had been crying, and her
manner is so excitable."

"She has been strange all day, almost
repellant. Felix called—and—I don't know
what happened, she insisted upon my leav-

ing her alone with him ; but I am afraid there was a scene of some sort. I know she had been crying, because her eyes were so red, but she would say nothing, and I was afraid to ask her."

" Better not. I hope she is not still thinking of that fellow Beauclerk. However——" he stops short and sighs heavily.

" You must not think of her now," says Barbara, quickly ; " your own trouble is enough for you. Were your brother's affairs so very bad that they necessitate the giving up of everything ? "

" It has been going on for years. My father has had to economise, to cut down everything. You know the old place was let to a Mr.—Mr.—I quite forget the name now," pressing his hand to his brow ; " a Manchester man at all events, but we always hoped my father would have been able to take it back from him next year, but now——"

" But you say they think in time that the property will——"

"*They* think so. I don't. But it would be a pity to undeceive them. I am afraid, Barbara," with a sad look at her, " you made a bad match. Even when the chance comes in your way to rise out of poverty it proves a thoroughly useless one."

" It isn't like you to talk like that," says she quickly. " There ! you are overwrought, and no wonder too. Come upstairs and let us see what you will want for your journey." Her tone has grown purposely brisk ; surely on an occasion such as this she is a wife, a companion in a thousand. " There must be many things to be considered ; both for you and for me. And the thing is, to take nothing unnecessary. Those foreign places, I hear, are so——"

" It hardly matters what I take," says he wearily.

" Well, it matters what *I* take," says she briskly. " Come and give me a help, Freddy. You know how I hate to have servants standing over me. Other people stand over their

servants, but they are poor rich people. I
like to see how the clothes are packed."
She is speaking not quite truthfully. Few
people like to be spared trouble so much
as she does, but it seems good in her eyes
now to rouse him from the melancholy that
is fast growing on him. " Come," she says,
tucking her arm into his.

CHAPTER IV.

> " It is not to-morrow; ah, were it to-day !
> There are two that I know that would be gay.
> Good-bye! Good-bye! Good-bye!
> Ah! parting wounds so bitterly !"

IT is six weeks later, " Spring has come up this way," and all the earth is glad with a fresh birth.

> " Tantarara! the joyous Book of Spring
> Lies open, writ in blossoms ; not a bird
> Of evil augury is seen or heard!
> Come now, like Pan's old crew we'll dance and sing,
> Or Oberon's, for hill and valley ring
> To March's bugle-horn—earth's blood is stirred.

March has indeed come ; boisterous, wild, terrible, in many ways, but lovely in others. There is a freshness in the air that rouses glad thoughts within the breast, vague thoughts, sweet, as undefinable, and that yet mean life. The whole land seems to have sprung up from a long slumber, and

to be looking with wide happy eyes upon
the fresh marvels Nature is preparing for
it. Rather naked she stands as yet, rub-
bing her sleepy lids, having just cast from
her her coat of snow, and feeling somewhat
bare in the frail garment of bursting leaves,
and timid grass growths, that as yet is all
she can find wherein to hide her charms;
but half clothed as she is, she is still beautiful.

Everything seems full of an eager triumph.
Hills, trees, valleys, lawns and bursting
streams, all are overflowing with a wild enjoyment. The dull, dingy drapery in which
Winter had shrouded them has now been
cast aside, and the resplendent furniture with
which each Spring delights to deck her home,
stands revealed.

All these past dead months her house has
lain desolate, enfolded in death's cerements,
but now uprising in her vigorous youth, she
flings aside the dull coverings, and lets the
sweet, brilliant hues that lie beneath, shine

forth in all their beauty to meet the eye of day.

Earth and sky are in bridal array, and from the rich recesses of the woods, and from each shrub and branch the soft glad pæans of the mating birds sound like a wedding chant.

Monkton had come back from that sad journey to Nice some weeks ago. He had had very little to tell on his return, and that of the saddest. It had all been only too true about those iniquitous debts ; and the old people were in great distress. The two town houses should be let at once, and the old place in Warwickshire—the *home*, as he had called it—well ! there was no hope now that it would ever be redeemed from the hands of the Manchester people who held it; and Sir George had been so sure that this Spring he would have been in a position to get back his own, and have the old place once more in his possession. It was all very sad.

" There is no hope now. He will have to let the place to Barton for the next ten years," said Monkton to his wife when he got home. Barton was the Manchester man. " He is still holding off about doing it, but he knows it must be done, and at all events the reality won't be a bit worse than the thinking about it. Poor old Governor ! You wouldn't know him, Barbara. He has gone to skin and bone, and such a frightened sort of look in his eyes."

" Oh ! poor, *poor* old man ! " cried Barbara, who could forget everything in the way of past unkindness where her sympathies were enlisted.

Towards the end of February the guests had begun to arrive at the Court. Lady Baltimore had returned there during January with her little son, but Baltimore had not put in an appearance for some weeks later. A good many new people unknown to the Monktons had arrived there with others who they did know, and after awhile Dicky

Browne had come and Miss Maliphant and the Brabazons and some others with whom Joyce was on friendly terms, but even though Lady Baltimore had made rather a point of the girl's being with her, Joyce had gone to her but sparingly, and always in fear and trembling. It was so impossible to know *who* might not have arrived last night, or was going to arrive *this* night!

Besides, Barbara and Freddy were so saddened, so upset by the late death and its consequences, that it seemed unkind even to pretend to enjoy oneself. Joyce grasped at this excuse to say "no" very often to Lady Baltimore's kindly longings to have her with her. That, up to this, neither Dysart nor Beauclerk had come to the Court, had been a comfort to her; but that they might come at any moment kept her watchful and uneasy. Indeed only yesterday she had heard from Lady Baltimore that both were expected during the ensuing week.

That news leaves her rather unstrung and nervous to-day. After luncheon, having successfully eluded Tommy the lynx-eyed, she decides upon going for a long walk with a view to working off the depression to which she has become prey. This is how she happens to be out of the way when the letter comes for Barbara that changes altogether the tenour of their lives.

The afternoon post brings it. The delicious Spring day has worn itself almost to a close when Monkton, entering his wife's room, where she is busy at a sewing machine, altering a frock for Mabel, drops a letter over her shoulder into her lap.

" What a queer-looking letter," says she, staring in amazement at the big official blue envelope.

" Ah—ha, I *thought* it would make you shiver," says he, lounging over to the fire and nestling his back comfortably against the mantelpiece. " What have *you* been up to, I should like to know. No wonder you are turning a lively purple."

"But what can it be?" says she.

"That's just it," says he teazingly. "I *hope* they aren't going to arrest you, that's all. Five years' penal servitude is not a thing to hanker after."

Mrs. Monkton, however, is not listening to this tirade. She has broken open the envelope and is now scanning hurriedly the contents of the important-looking document within. There is a pause—a lengthened one. . . . Presently Barbara rises from her seat, mechanically as it were, always with her eyes fixed on the letter in her hand. She has grown a little pale—a little puzzled frown is contracting her forehead.

"Freddy!" says she in a rather strange tone.

"What?" says he quickly. "No *more* bad news I hope."

"Oh no! Oh *yes!* I can't make it out —but—I'm afraid my poor uncle is dead."

" Your uncle ? "

" Yes, yes. My father's brother. I think I told you about him. He went abroad years ago, and we—Joyce and I—believed him dead a long time ago, long before I married *you* even—but now——. Come here and read it. It is worded so oddly that it puzzles me."

" Let me see it," says Monkton.

He sinks into an easy chair, and drags her down on to his knee, the better to see over her shoulder. Thus satisfactorily arranged, he begins to read rapidly the letter she holds up before his eyes.

" Yes, dead indeed," says he *sotto voce.* " Go on, turn over ; you mustn't fret about *that* you know, Barbara—er—er——" reading. " What's this ? *By* Jove ! "

" What ? " says his wife anxiously. " What is the meaning of this horrid letter, Freddy ? "

" There are a few people who might not call it horrid," says Monkton, placing his arm round her, and rising from the chair.

He is looking very grave. " Even though it brings you news of your poor uncle's death, still—it brings you too the information that you are heiress to about a quarter of a million ! "

" What ! " says Barbara faintly. And then, " Oh *no*. Oh ! nonsense ! there must be some mistake ! "

" Well, it *sounds* like it at all events. ' Sad occurrence,' h'm—h'm——" reading. " ' Co-heiresses. Very considerable fortune.' " He looks to the signature of the letter. " Hodgson and Fair. Very respectable firm ! My father has had dealings with them. They say your uncle died in Sydney, and has left behind him an immense sum of money. Half a million, in fact, to which you and Joyce are co-heiresses."

" There must be a mistake," repeats Barbara, in a low tone. " It seems too like a fairy tale."

" It does. And yet, lawyers like Hodgson and Fair are not likely to be led into a *cul-de-*

sac. If——" he pauses, and looks earnestly at his wife. " If it does prove true, Barbara, you will be a very rich woman."

" And you will be rich *with* me," says she, quickly, in an agitated tone. " But, but——"

" Yes ; it does seem difficult to believe," interrupts he, slowly. " What a letter ! " His eyes fall on it again, and she, drawing close to him, 'reads it once more, carefully.

" I think there is truth in it," says she, at last. " It sounds more like being all right, more *reasonable,* when read a second time. Freddy——"

She steps a little bit away from him, and rests her beautiful eyes full on his.

" Have you thought," says she, slowly, " that if there is truth in this story, how much we shall be able to do for your father and mother ! "

Monkton starts as if stung. For *them.* To do anything for them. For the two who had so wantonly offended and insulted her during all her married life. Is her first thought to be for *them?*

"Yes, yes," says she, eagerly. "We shall be able to help them out of all their difficulties. Oh! I didn't *say* much to you, but their grief, their troubles, have gone to my very heart. I couldn't *bear* to think of their being obliged to give up their houses, their comforts, and in their old age, too! Now, we shall be able to smooth matters for them!"

CHAPTER V.

" It's we two, it's we two, it's we two for aye,
   All the world and we two, and Heaven be our stay,
   Like a laverock in the lift, sing, O bonny bride!
   All the world was Adam once, with Eve by his side."

THE light in her eyes is angelic. She has laid her hands upon both her husband's arms, as if expecting him to take her into them as he always does only too gladly on the smallest provocation. Just now, he fails her—for the moment only, however.

" Barbara," says he, in a choked voice ; he holds her from him, examining her face critically. His thoughts are painful, yet proud—proud beyond telling. His examination does not last long ; there is nothing but good to be read in that fair, sweet, lovable face. He gathers her to him with a force that is almost hurtful.

" Are you a woman at all, or just an
angel ? " says he with a deep sigh.

" What is it, Freddy ? "

" After all they have done to you. Their
insults, coldness, *abominable* conduct, to think
that your first thought should be for them.
Why look here, Barbara," vehemently, " they
are not worthy that you should——"

" Tut ! " interrupts she, lightly, yet with a
little sob in her throat. His praise is so sweet
to her. " You over-rate me. Is it for them I
would do it or for *you?* There, take all the
thought for yourself. And, besides, are not
you and I one, and shall not your people be
my people. Come, if you think of it, there is
no such great merit after all."

" You forget——"

" No ; not a word against them. I won't
listen," thrusting her fingers into her ears.
" It is all over and done with long ago.
And it is our turn now, and let us do things
decently, and in order, and create no heart-
burnings."

" But when I think——"

" If thinking makes you look like that, *don't* think."

" But I must. I must remember how they scorned and slighted you. It never seems to have come home to me so vividly as now—now when you seem to have forgotten it. Oh, Barbara ! " He presses back her head and looks long and tenderly into her eyes. " I was not mistaken, indeed, when I gave you my heart. Surely you are one amongst ten thousand."

" Silly boy," says she, with a little tremulous laugh ; glad to her very soul's centre, however, because of his words. " What is there to praise me for ? Have I not warned you that I am purely selfish ? What is there I would not do for very love of you ? Come, Freddy," shaking herself loose from him, and laughing now with honest delight. " Let us be reasonable. Oh ! poor old uncle, it seems hateful to rejoice thus over his death, but his memory is really only a shadow after all, and

I suppose he meant to make us happy by his
gift, eh, Freddy?"

"Yes. How well he remembered during
all these years. He could have formed no
other ties."

"None, naturally." Short pause. "There
is that black mare of Mike Donovan's, Freddy,
that you so fancied. You can buy it now."

Monkton laughs involuntarily. Something
of the child has always lingered about
Barbara.

"And I should like to get a black velvet
gown," says she, her face brightening, "and
to buy Joyce a—— Oh! but Joyce will be
rich herself."

"Yes. I'm really afraid you will be done
out of the joy of overloading Joyce with gifts ;
she'll be able to give *you* something. That
will be a change at all events. As for the
velvet gown, if this," touching the letter,
" bears any meaning, I should think you need
not confine yourself to *one* velvet gown."

"And there's Tommy," says she quickly,

her thoughts running so quickly that she scarcely hears him. "You have always said you wanted to put him in the army. Now you can do it."

"Yes," says Monkton, with sudden interest. "I *should* like that. But you—you shrank from the thought, didn't you."

"Well, he might have to go to India," says she nervously.

"And what of that?"

"Oh, nothing—that is nothing really—only there are lions and tigers there, Freddy; *aren't* there now?"

"One or two," says Mr. Monkton, "if we are to believe travellers' tales. But they are all proverbially false. I don't believe in lions at all, myself. I'm sure they are myths. Well, let him go into the navy then. Lions and tigers don't as a rule inhabit the great deep."

"Oh, no; but *sharks* do," says she, with a visible shudder. "No, no, on the whole I had rather trust him to the beasts of the field. He could run away from them, but you *can't* run in the sea."

"True," says Mr. Monkton, with exemplary gravity. "I couldn't at all events."

*   *   *   *   *

Monkton had to run across to London about the extraordinary legacy left to his wife and Joyce. But further investigation proved the story true. The money was, indeed, there, and they were the only heirs. From being distinctly poor, they rose to the height of a very respectable income, and Monkton being in town, where the old Monktons still were, also was commanded by his wife to go to them and pay off their largest liabilities— debts contracted by the dead son, and to so arrange that they should not be at the necessity of leaving themselves houseless.

The Manchester people who had taken the old place in Warwickshire were now informed that they could not have it beyond the term agreed upon, but about this the old people had something to say too. They would not take back the family place. They had but one son now, and the sooner he went to live there the better. Lady Monkton, completely broken down and melted by Barbara's generosity, went so far as to send her a long letter, telling her it would be the dearest wish of her and Sir George's hearts that *she* should preside as mistress over the beautiful old homestead, and that it would give them great happiness to imagine the children — the *grandchildren* — running riot through the big wainscoted rooms. Barbara was not to wait for her—Lady Monkton's— death to take up her position as head of the house. She was to go to Warwickshire at once, the moment those detestable Manchester people were out of it, and Lady Monkton, if Barbara would be so good as to make her welcome, would like to come to her for three months every year, to see the children and her son, and her *daughter!* The last was the crowning touch. For the rest, Barbara

was not to hesitate about accepting the
Warwickshire place, as Lady Monkton and
Sir George were devoted to Town life, and
never felt quite well when away from smoky
London.

This last was true. As a fact the old
people were thoroughly imbued with a desire
for the turmoil of city life, and the three
months of country Lady Monkton had stipu-
lated for, were quite as much as they desired
of rustic felicity.

Barbara accepted the gift of the old home.
Eventually, of course, it would be hers, but
she knew the old people meant the present
giving of it as a sort of return for her
liberality—for the generosity that had enabled
them to once more lift their heads amongst
their equals.

*   *   *   *   *

The great news meanwhile had spread
like wildfire through the Irish county
where the Frederic Monktons lived. Lady

Baltimore was unfeignedly glad about it, and came down at once to embrace Barbara, and say all sorts of delightful things about it. The excitement of the whole affair seemed to dissipate all the sadness and depression that had followed on the death of the elder son, and nothing now was talked of but the great good luck that had fallen into the paths of Barbara and Joyce. The poor old uncle had been considered dead for so many years previously, and was indeed such a dim memory to his nieces that it would have been the purest affectation to pretend to feel any deep grief for his demise.

Perhaps what grieved Barbara most of all, though she said very little about it, was the idea of having to leave the old house in which they were now living. It did not cheer her to think of the place in Warwickshire, which, of course, was beautiful, and full of possibilities.

This foolish old Irish home—rich in discomforts—*was* home. It seemed hard to

abandon it.   It was not a palatial mansion,
certainly ; it was even dismal in many ways,
but it contained more love in its little space
than many a noble mansion could boast.   It
seemed cruel—ungrateful—to cast it behind
her, once it was possible to her to mount a
few steps higher on the rungs of the worldly
ladder.

How happy they had all been here together,
in this foolish old house that every severe
storm seemed to threaten with final disso-
lution.   It gave her many a secret pang to
think that she must part from it for ever
before another year should dawn.

*   *   *   *   *

CHAPTER VI.

"Looks the heart alone discover,
    If the tongue its thoughts can tell,
'Tis in vain you play the lover,
    You have never *felt* the spell."

JOYCE, who had been dreading, with a silent
but terrible fear, her first meeting with
Dysart, had found it no such great matter
after all when at last they were face to face.
Dysart had met her as coolly, with apparently
as little concern as though no former pas-
sages had ever taken place between them.

His manner was perfectly calm, and as
devoid of feeling as anyone could desire, and
it was open to her comprehension that he
avoided her whenever he possibly could. She
told herself this was all she could, or did,
desire ; yet, nevertheless, she writhed beneath the certainty of it.

Beauclerk had not arrived until a week

later than Dysart; until, indeed, the news
of the marvellous fortune that had come to
her was well authenticated, and then had
been all that could possibly be expected of
him. His manner was perfect. He still sat
and gazed with delightfully friendly eyes
into Miss Maliphant's pleased countenance,
and anon skimmed across room or lawn to
whisper beautiful nothings to Miss Kavanagh.
The latter's change of fortune did not, apparently, seem to affect him in the least.
After all, even now, she was not so good a
parti as Miss Maliphant where money was
concerned, but then there were other things.
Whatever his outward manner might lead
one to suspect, beyond doubt he thought a
great deal at this time, and finally came to
a conclusion.

Joyce's fortune had helped *her* in many
ways; it had helped many of the poor around
her too, but it did even more than that—
it helped Mr. Beauclerk to make up his mind
with regard to his matrimonial prospects.

Sitting in his chambers in Town with Lady Baltimore's letter before him that told him of the change in Joyce's fortune — of the fortune that had changed her, in fact, from a pretty, penniless girl to a pretty, rich one, he told himself that, after all, she had certainly been the girl for *him*, since the commencement of their acquaintance.

She was charming—not a whit more now than then. He would not belie his own taste so far as to admit that she was more desirable in any way now, in her prosperity, than when first he saw her, and paid her the immense compliment of admiring her.

He permitted himself to grow a little enthusiastic, however, to say out loud to himself as it were, all that he had hardly allowed himself to think up to this. She was, beyond question, *the* most charming girl in the world! Such grace—such finish! A girl worthy of the love of the best of men —presumably himself!

He had always loved her—always! He

had never felt so sure of that delightful
fact as *now*. He had had a kind of knowledge, even when afraid to give ear to it,
that she was the wife best suited to him to
be found anywhere. She *understood* him!
They were thoroughly *en rapport* with each
other. Their marriage would be a success
in the deepest, sincerest meaning of that
word.

He leant luxuriously amongst the cushions
of his chair, lit a fragrant cigarette, and ran
his mind backwards over many things.
Well! *Perhaps* so! But yet if he *had* re-
frained from proposing to her until now—
now when Fate smiles upon her—it was
simply because he dreaded dragging her into
a marriage where she could not have had
all those little best things of life that so
peerless a creature had every right to demand.

Yes! It was for her sake alone he had
hesitated. He feels sure of that now. He
has thoroughly persuaded himself of the

purity of the motives that kept him tongue-
tied when honour called aloud to him for
speech. He feels himself so exalted that he
metaphorically pats himself upon the back
and tells himself he is a righteous being—
a very Brutus where honour is concerned ;
any other man might have hurried that
exquisite creature into a squalid marriage
for the mere sake of gratifying an over-
powering affection, but *he* had been above
all that ! He had considered *her !* The
man's duty is ever to protect the woman !
He had protected *her* — even from herself ;
for that she would have been only too willing to link her sweet fate with his at any
price, was patent to all the world. Few
people have felt as virtuous as Mr. Beauclerk as he comes to the end of *this* thread
of his imaginings.

Well ! He will make it up to her ! He
smiles benignly through the smoke that rises
round his nose. She shall never have reason
to remember that he had not fallen on his

knees to her—as a less considerate man
might have done—when he was without the
means to make her life as bright as it
should be.

The most eager of lovers must live, and
eating is the first move towards that conclusion.   Yet if he had given way to selfish
desires they would scarcely, he and she,
have had sufficient bread (of any delectable
kind) to fill their mouths.   But now, all
would be different.   She, clever girl ! had
supplied the blank ; she had squared the
difficulty.   Having provided the wherewithal
to keep body and soul together in a nice,
respectable, fashionable, modern sort of way,
her constancy shall certainly be rewarded.
He will go straight down to the Court, and
declare to her the sentiments that have been
warming his breast (silently !) all these past
months.   What a *dear* girl she is, and so
fond of him.   That in itself is an extra
charm in her very delightful character.
And those fortunate thousands !   Quite a

quarter of a million, isn't it ? Well, of
course, no use saying they won't come in
handy—no use being hypocritical over it—
horrid thing a hypocrite !—well, those
thousands naturally have their charm too.

He rose ; flung his cigarette aside (it was
finished as far as careful enjoyment would
permit) and rang for his servant to pack his
portmanteaux. He was going to the Court
by the morning train.

*   *   *   *   *

Now that he is here, however, he restrains
the ardour that no doubt is consuming him,
with altogether admirable patience, and waits
for the chance that may permit him to lay
his valuable affections at Joyce's feet. A
dinner to be followed by an impromptu
dance at the Court suggests itself as a very
fitting opportunity. He grasps it. Yes, to-
morrow evening will be an excellent and
artistic opening for a thing of this sort.
All through luncheon, even whilst convers-

ing with Joyce and Miss Maliphant on various outside topics, his versatile mind is arranging a picturesque spot in the garden enclosures wherein to make Joyce a happy woman !

Lady Swansdown, glancing across the table at him, laughs lightly. Always disliking him, she has still been able to read him very clearly, and his determination to now propose to Joyce amuses her nearly as much as it annoys her. Frivolous to the last degree as she is, an honest regard for Joyce has taken hold within her breast. Lady Baltimore too is disturbed by her brother's present attitude, yet a feeling that Joyce is equal to the struggle comforts her. She sighs, however, as she looks at her. Life to Lady Baltimore has become a terrible thing. It was bad before—but now —*lately*—— It is vain to try to conceal from herself that the flirtation between her husband and her whilom friend, Lady Swansdown, is gaining ground every day.

A sad and scornful submission to her fate is all that is left her, and yet—it is so hard to submit.

Perhaps, of all those round her, Dicky Browne is the one who sees most of Lady Baltimore's trouble, and whilst disbelieving in any very serious attachment between Baltimore and Lady Swansdown, is still secretly incensed at the indignity put upon Isabel, of whom he is extremely fond in his own odd, desultory way. He had even gone so far yesterday as to hint about it to Beauclerk, who as Lady Baltimore's brother might, he thought, reasonably be supposed to have her interests at heart.

In this, however, he found himself lamentably mistaken. Beauclerk had stared at him in a gentlemanly sort of way, as if he had seven heads. He seemed, indeed, horrified at Dicky's bad taste in bringing up an affair of this kind to the common light of day ; such an ordinary affair too ! What the deuce did the fellow mean ?

"*You* should interfere," said Dicky Browne stoutly, unimpressed by the gentlemanly stare. "A word or two to Baltimore would arrange it. I don't believe he cares a screw about—the other."

"My dear fellow, I *never* interfere !" said Beauclerk icily, whereon Dicky, with an indignant twist of his shoulder, had left him.

Something at luncheon to-day, a little touch of coquetry on the part of Lady Swansdown, had set his anger going again. And an hour later, happening to pass through one of the conservatories he is still further incensed by a vision of Baltimore leaning over Lady Swansdown in a half careless, half lover-like attitude. Even as Dicky hesitates whether to withdraw noiselessly, or bring a flower-pot to the ground with a loud clangour, Baltimore stooping, presses his lips to his pretty companion's hand, and with a light laugh runs down the conservatory steps to the garden outside.

Dicky, after a second's consideration, goes

forward, and almost before Lady Swansdown has time to realize his approach drops into the seat just vacated by Baltimore.

"I say," says he deliberately, "I'd chuck it up if I were you."

"Would you?" says Lady Swansdown with admirable unconcern, though her heart has begun to beat with some rapidity. "Chuck up what, however? My acquaintance with *you*?"

"Not a bit of it," says Mr. Browne quite as coolly, being unmoved by this counter attack, "you daren't do that. I shouldn't survive it, and I suppose you don't want to have murder on your soul. However, as that dear old frugal proverb advises us, to waste nothing, lest we should want it later on, I'll allow your question to stand, merely suggesting that you should substitute for my name that of Baltimore! If you will put it again *that* way, I'll say 'yes' to it."

Lady Swansdown laughs, but the laugh

is vague, a little overdone; and without the
usual ring.

"I should hate to think your intellect
was failing," says she. "But is there any
meaning in your words?"

"A great deal," says Mr. Browne suavely.
He draws his chair rather closer to hers.

"Yes? Really? I am afraid, however,
you would have to alter more words than
the one you mention. 'Acquaintance' for
example. That might do very well where
you are concerned, but I assure you what
I feel for Lord Baltimore is sincere friendship."

"Is it?" says Dicky mildly. "That's a
little rough on me, isn't it? especially as
you *know* I'm very devoted to you; whereas
Baltimore—is he devoted to you?"

This barbed arrow reaches its home.
Lady Swansdown's colour grows more
brilliant, and then fades away into nothing-
ness. She is now indeed very pale.

"You mean——?" says she slowly.

"Hardly anything," says he. "The whole thing really is not worth a discussion —but——"

"Go on," says she with a little impatient frowning glance. "You think that——"

"I don't *think* about it," says Mr. Browne plaintively, "I know what I am speaking about. All the world knows it too."

"Knows *what?* Take care, Dicky!" says she with a flash from her large eyes.

"That I adore you!" says Mr. Browne with a mournful shake of his head. "Hopelessly, I admit, whereas Baltimore——"

"Well?" with a short, but now unmistakable touch of defiance.

"All the world knows too—at least the intelligent part of it—that he is silly enough to adore his own wife! A pity this fact has not come home to him! Really he goes about as if he were ignorant of it."

Lady Swansdown leans back in her chair,

and a rather wild little burst of mirth breaks from her.

"And *she?*" she asks, with a sidelong glance at Dicky.

"Isabel, you mean? Give her a chance," says he slowly, earnestly.

"Ah! you would appeal to me after deriding me?"

"I would only remind you that you have a good heart," says he quickly. "As for Baltimore, he is a fool."

"Well, you are not so," says she with a bitter little laugh. "And now — do you think you could go away, Dicky? I confess I have had enough of you and your smart sayings, for a little while at all events."

"Why don't you say at once that you want to go to sleep," says Mr. Browne, ignoring cleverly her agitation. "Women always go to sleep, don't they, when they are left alone? I expect you want to slip up to your room, and get an extra beauty sleep, so as to eclipse all the others this evening. Rather mean of you isn't it—considering you can do it without any trouble ? *You* want nothing."

" For once you are at fault," says she, looking at him through half lowered lids. Her beautiful lips have taken a contemptuous curve, yet in reality the contempt is more for herself than her companion.

" Never mind, one likes new sensations," says Dicky cheerfully. "However, I still cling to my first belief, and I may as well give you before I go a home-thrust."

" What, another ? " says she smiling indifferently.

" A *first* surely."

" Well, what is it ? You are so bent on being unpleasant that it would be a pity to prevent you. *Do* say it and get it over," says she with a shrug. He always wondered afterwards why she had borne with him so long.

" In what mad haste to be rid of me,"

says he, rising to his feet, tearful reproach
in his voice. "Hear me then! I think it
cruel of you, who are peerless amongst your
fellows, to seek to gain an advantage over
another." He pauses—long enough to know
that she quite understands him. "Nature
has given you so many charms, that you
can afford to be magnanimous."

"Nature has given me amongst them
an excellent temper," says she indolently
"*You*, at all events, must admit that. As
for my charms—really, where are they?
Of what use are they to me? Barren—
all barren! They bring me no luck."

"They have brought you *me!*" says Mr.
Browne, with heavy emphasis.

"Ah!" says she, with emphasis of her
own quite as heavy, "that's what I say;
they have brought me—no luck:" this is
unkind. "Good Dicky," says she languidly,
"*may* I be alone for a while?"

"After *that*, certainly, so far as I am
concerned," says Mr. Browne, rising with

all the appearance of one wounded to the
death. " Still, a last word," says he. " If
you *must* snooze, don't do it *here*, I be-
seech you ; people come and go and——"

" Be happy about that. I shan't sleep
here or anywhere else," interrupts she, a
little sadly perhaps in spite of her laughing mouth. " There *go* ! Let me forget
you and your platitudes for a while if I can."

She waves him from her, and sinking
back into the cosy chair in which she is
sitting, gives way to one cankering thought.

CHAPTER VII.

> " Love took up the harp of life, and smote on all the
> chords with might,
> Smote the chord of Self, that, trembling, passed in
> music out of sight."

SHE is startled into a remembrance of the
present by the entrance of somebody. After
all, Dicky the troublesome was right. *This*
is no spot in which to sleep or dream in.
Turning her head with an indolent impa-
tience, to see who has come to disturb her,
she meets Lady Baltimore's clear eyes.

Some sharp pang of remorse, or *fear*
perhaps, compels her to spring to her feet,
and gaze at her hostess with an expression
that is almost defiant. Dicky's words so
far had taken effect, that she now dreads
and *hates* to meet the woman who once
had been her staunch friend.

Lady Baltimore, unable to ignore the look

in her rival's eyes, still advances towards
her with unfaltering step. Perhaps a touch
of disdain, of contempt, is perceptible in
her own gaze because Lady Swansdown,
paling, moves towards *her*. She seems to
have lost all self-control. She is trembling
violently ; it is a crisis.

"What is it ? " says Lady Swansdown
harshly. " Why do you look at me like
that ? Has it come to a close between us,
Isabel ? Oh, if so," vehemently, " it is *better*
so."

" I don't think I understand you," says
Lady Baltimore, who has grown very white.
Her tone is haughty, she has drawn back
a little as if to escape from contact with
the other.

" Ah, that is so like you," says Lady
Swansdown with a rather fierce little laugh.
" You pretend, pretend, pretend, from morning till night. You entrench yourself behind
your pride, and——"

" You know what you are doing, Beatrice?" says Lady Baltimore, ignoring this outburst completely, and speaking in a calm level tone, yet with a face like marble.

"Yes, and you know too," says Lady Swansdown. Then with an overwhelming vehemence, "Why don't you do something? Why don't you assert yourself?"

"I shall *never* assert myself," says Lady Baltimore slowly.

"You mean that whatever comes you will not interfere."

"That, exactly," turning her eyes full on the other's face with a terrible disdain. "I shall never interfere in this—or *any other* of his flirtations."

It is a sharp stab! Lady Swansdown winces visibly.

"What a woman you are," cries she. "Have you ever thought of it, Isabel? You are unjust to him, unfair. You," passionately, "treat him as though he were the dust beneath your feet, and yet you expect him to remain immaculate for your sake, pure as an acolyte — a thing of ice——"

" No," coldly. " You mistake me. I know too much of him to expect perfection, nay, common decency, from him. But *you*, it was *you* whom I hoped to find immaculate."

" You expect too much then. One iceberg in your midst is enough, and that you have kindly supplied in your own person. Put me out of the discussion altogether."

" Ah, you have made that impossible. I cannnot do that. I have known you too long, I have liked you too well. I have," with a swift, but terrible, glance at her, "*loved you!*"

" *Isabel!* "

" No, *no*, not a word. It is too late now."

" True," says Lady Swansdown, bringing back the arms she had extended, and letting them fall with a sudden dull vehemence to her sides. Her agitation is uncontrolled.

"That was so long ago, that no doubt you have forgotten all about it. You," bitterly, "have forgotten a good deal."

"And you," says Lady Baltimore very calmly. "What is it you have *not* forgotten —your self-respect," deliberately, "amongst other things."

"Take care, take care!" says Lady Swansdown in a low tone. She has turned furiously upon her.

"Why should I take care?" She throws up her small head scornfully. "Have I said one word too much?"

"Too much indeed!" says Lady Swansdown distinctly, but faintly. She turns her head, but not her eyes, in Isabel's direction. "I am afraid you will have to endure me for one day longer," she says in a low voice. "After that, you shall bid me a farewell that will last for ever!"

"You have come to a wise decision," says Lady Baltimore, immovably.

There is something so contemptuous in

her whole bearing that it maddens the other.

"How *dare* you speak to me like that?" cries she with sudden violence, not to be repressed. "*You*, of all others! Do you think you are not in fault at all?—that you stand blameless before the world?"

The blood has flamed into her pale cheeks, her eyes are on fire. She advances towards Lady Baltimore with such a passion of angry despair in look and tone, that involuntarily the latter retreats before her.

"*Who* shall blame me?" demands Lady Baltimore haughtily.

"I—I for one. "Icicle that you are, how can you know what love means? You have no heart to feel, no longing to forgive. And what has he done to you—nothing, *nothing* that any other woman would not gladly condone."

"You are a partisan," says Lady Baltimore coldly. "You would plead his cause

and to *me*. You are violent, but that does
not put you in the right. What do *you*
know of Baltimore that I do not know?
By what right do you defend him?"

"There is such a thing as friendship."

"Is there?" says the other with deep
meaning. "*Is* there, Beatrice? Oh think,
think!" A little bitter smile curls the
corners of her lips. "That *you* should ad-
vocate the cause of friendship to *me*," says
she, her words falling with cruel scorn, one
by one, slowly from her lips.

"You think me false," says Lady Swansdown. She is terribly agitated. "There
was an old friendship between us. I know
that—I *feel* it; you think me altogether
false to it?"

"I think of you as little as I can help,"
says Isabel contemptuously. "Why should
I waste a thought on you?"

"True. Why indeed! One so capable of
controlling her emotions as you are, need
never give way to superfluous or useless

thoughts. Still, give one to Baltimore. It is our last conversation together, therefore bear with me—hear me. All his sins lie in the past. He——"

" You must be *mad* to talk to me like this," interrupts Isabel, flushing crimson. " Has he asked you to intercede for him ? *Could* even *he* go so far as that ? Is it a last insult ? What are *you* to him, that you thus adopt his cause ? *Answer* me ! " cries she imperiously ; all her coldness, all her stern determination to suppress herself seems broken up.

" Nothing ! " returns Lady Swansdown, becoming calmer as she notes the other's growing vehemence. " I never shall be anything. I have but one excuse for my interference——" She pauses.

" And that ? "

" *I love him !* " steadily but faintly. Her eyes have sought the ground.

" *Ah !* " says Lady Baltimore.

" It is true," slowly. " It is equally true

—that he—does not love me. Let me then speak. All his sins, believe me, lie behind him. That woman, that friend of yours, who told you of his renewed acquaintance with Madame Istray, lied to you! There was no truth in what she said."

"I can quite understand *your* not wishing to believe in that story," says Lady Baltimore with an undisguised sneer.

"Like all good women you can take pleasure in inflicting a wound," says Lady Swansdown, controlling herself admirably; "but do not let your detestation of me blind you to the fact that my words contain truth. If you will listen, I can——"

"Not a word," says Lady Baltimore, making a movement with her hand as if to efface the other. "I will have none of your confidences."

"It seems to me," quickly, "you are determined *not* to believe."

"You are at liberty to think as you will."

" The time may come when you will regret you did not listen to me to-day."

" Is that a threat ? "

" No ; but I am going. There will be no further opportunity for you to hear me."

" You must pardon me if I say that I am glad of that," says Lady Baltimore, her very lips white. " I could have borne little more. *Do* what you will. *Go* where you will, with *whom* you will " (with deliberate insult), " but at least spare me a repetition of such a scene as this."

She turns, and with an indescribably haughty gesture leaves the room.

CHAPTER VIII.

"The name of the slough was Despond."

DANCING is going on in the small drawing-room. A few night broughams are still arriving, and young girls, accompanied by their brothers only, are making the room look lovely. It is quite an impromptu affair, quite informal. Dicky Browne, altogether in his element, is flitting from flower to flower, saying beautiful nothings to any of the girls who are kind enough or silly enough to waste a moment on so irreclaimable a butterfly.

He is not so entirely engrossed by his pleasing occupation, however, as to be lost to the more serious matters that are going on around him. He is specially struck by the fact that Lady Swansdown, who had been in charming spirits all through the afternoon, and afterwards at dinner, is now dancing a great deal with Beauclerk—of all people—and making herself, apparently, very delightful to him. His own personal belief up to this had been that she detested Beauclerk, and now, to see her smiling upon him and favouring him with waltz after waltz, upsets Dicky's powers of penetration to an almost fatal extent.

"I wonder what the deuce she's up to now," says he to himself, leaning against the wall behind him, and giving voice unconsciously to the thoughts within him.

"Eh," says somebody at his ear.

He looks round hastily to find Miss Maliphant has come to anchor on his left, and that her eyes too are directed on Beauclerk, who, with Lady Swansdown, is standing at the lower end of the room.

"Eh, to *you*," says he brilliantly.

"I always rather fancied that Mr. Beauclerk and Lady Swansdown were antipathetic," says Miss Maliphant in her usual heavy downright way.

"There was room for it," says Mr. Browne gloomily.

"For it?"

"Your fancy."

"Yes; so *I* think. Lady Swansdown has always seemed to me to be rather—rather—Eh?"

"Decidedly so," agrees Mr. Browne. "And as for Beauclerk, *he* is quite too dreadfully 'rather,' don't you think?"

"I don't know, I'm sure. He has often seemed to me a little *light*, but only on the surface."

"You've read him," says Mr. Browne with a confidential nod; "light on the surface, but deep, deep as a draw-well!"

"I don't think I mean what you do," says Miss Maliphant quickly. "However, we are not discussing Mr. Beauclerk, beyond the fact that I wonder to see him so genial with Lady Swansdown. They *used* to be thoroughly antagonistic, and *now*——why they seem quite good friends, don't they?

Quite thick, eh ? " with her usual graceful phraseology.

" Thick as thieves in Vallambrosa ? " says Mr. Browne with increasing gloom. Miss Maliphant turns to regard him doubtfully.

" *Leaves*," suggests she.

" *Thieves*," persists he immovably.

" Oh ! Ah ! It's a joke, perhaps," says she, the doubt growing.

Mr. Browne fixes a stern eye upon her.

" Is thy servant a dog ? " says he, and stalks indignantly away, leaving Miss Maliphant in the throes of uncertainty.

" Yet I'm *sure* it wasn't the right word," says she to herself, with a gathering frown of perplexity. " However, I may be wrong. I often *am*. And after all, Spain, we're told, is full of 'em."

Whether "thieves" or "leaves," she doesn't explain ; and presently indeed her mind wanders entirely away from Mr. Browne's maunderings to the subject that so much more nearly interests her. Beauclerk has not been quite so *empressé* in his manner to her to-night—not so altogether delightful. He has indeed, it seems to her, shirked her society a good deal, and has not been so assiduous about the scribbling of his name upon her card as usual; and then this sudden friendship with Lady Swansdown—what does *she* mean?

If she had only known. If the answer to her latter question had been given to her, her mind would have grown easier, and the idea of Lady Swansdown in the form of a rival would have been laid at rest for ever.

As a fact Lady Swansdown hardly understands herself to-night. That scene with her hostess has upset her mentally and bodily, and created in her a wild desire to get away from *herself*—and from Baltimore—at any cost. Some idle freak has induced her to use Beauclerk (who is detestable to her) as a safeguard from both, and he, unsettled in his own mind, and eager to come to conclusions with Joyce and her fortune, has lent himself to the wiles of his whilom foe, and is permitting himself to be charmed by her fascinating, if vagrant, mood.

Perhaps in all her life Lady Swansdown has never looked so lovely as to-night. Excitement and mental disturbance have lent a dangerous brilliancy to her eyes, a touch of colour to her cheek. There is something electric about her that moves those who gaze on her, and warns herself that a crisis is at hand.

Up to this she has been able to elude all Baltimore's attempts at conversation—has refused all his demands for a dance. Yet, the sure knowledge that the night will not go by without a *dénouement* of some kind between her and him is terribly present to her.

To-night ! The last night she will ever see him, in all human probability ! The exaltation that enables her to endure this thought is fraught with such agony that, brave and determined as she is, it is almost too much for her.

Yet *she*—Isabel—she should learn that
that old friendship between them was no
fable. To-night it would bear fruit. False,
she believed her— ! Well, she should see.

In a way, she clung to Beauclerk as a
means of escaping Baltimore. Throwing out
a thousand wiles to chain him to her side,
and succeeding. Three times she had given
a smiling "No," to Lord Baltimore's demand
for a dance, and regardless of opinion had
flung herself into a wild and open flirtation
with Beauclerk.

But it is growing towards midnight, and
her strength is failing her. These people—
will they *never* go? Will she never be
able to seek her own room, and solitude, and
despair, without calling down comment on
her head, and giving Isabel, that cold woman,
the chance of sneering at her weakness?

A sudden sense of the uselessness of it
all has taken possession of her. Her heart
sinks. It is at this moment that Baltimore
once more comes up to her.

" This dance ? " says he. " It is half-way through. You are not engaged, I suppose, as you are sitting down. May I have what remains of it ? "

She makes a little gesture of acquiescence, and rising, places her hand upon his arm.

CHAPTER IX.

"O life ! thou art a galling load
Along a rough, a weary road,
To wretches such as I."

THE crisis has come, she tells herself with a rather grim smile. Well, better have it and get it over.

That there had been a violent scene between Baltimore and his wife after dinner had somehow become known to her, and the marks of it still betray themselves in the former's frowning brow and sombre eyes.

It had been more of a scene than usual. Lady Baltimore, generally so calm, had for once lost herself, and given way to a passion of indignation that had shaken her to her very heart's core. Though so apparently unmoved, and almost insolent in her demeanour towards Lady Swansdown during their interview, she had been, nevertheless, cruelly wounded by it, and could not forgive Baltimore in that he had been its cause.

As for him, he could not forgive her all she had said and looked. With a heart on fire he had sought Lady Swansdown, the one woman whom he knew understood and believed in him. It was a perilous moment, and Beatrice knew it. She knew too that angry despair was driving him into her arms, not honest affection. She was strong enough to face this, and refuse to deceive herself about it.

"I didn't think you and Beauclerk had anything in common," says Baltimore, seating himself beside her on the low lounge that is half hidden from the public gaze by the Indian curtains that fall at each side of it. He had made no pretence of finishing the dance. He had led the way, and she had suffered herself to be led into the small ante-room that, half smothered in early spring flowers, lay off the dancing room.

"Ah! you see you have yet much to learn about me," says she with an attempt at gaiety—that fails however.

"About you—no!" says he almost defiantly. "Don't tell me I have deceived myself about you, Beatrice. You are all I have left to fall back upon now." His tone is reckless to the last degree.

"A forlorn *pis-aller*," says she steadily, with a forced smile. "What is it, Cyril?" —looking at him with sudden intentness— "Something has happened? *What?*"

"The old story," returns he. "And I am sick of it. I have thrown up my hand. I *would* have been faithful to her, Beatrice, I swear that—but—she does not care for my devotion. And as for me—now——" He throws out his arms as if tired to death, and draws in his breath heavily.

"Now?" says she leaning forward.

"Am I worth your acceptance?" says he, turning sharply to her. "I hardly dare to think it, and yet—you have been kind to me—and your own lot is not an altogether happy one—and——"

He pauses.

" Do you hesitate ? " asks she very bitterly, although her pale lips are smiling.

" Will you risk it all ? " says he sadly. " Will you come away with me ? I feel I have no friend on earth but you. Will you take pity on me ? I shall not stay here, whatever happens. I have striven against Fate too long—it has overcome me. Another land—a different life—complete forgetfulness——"

" Do you know what you are saying ? " asks Lady Swansdown, who has grown deadly white.

" Yes. I have thought it all out. It is for you now to decide. I have sometimes thought I was not entirely indifferent to you, and, at all events, we are friends in the best sense of the term. If you were a happy married woman, Beatrice, I should not speak

to you like this, but as it is—in another land
—if you will come with me—we——"

" Think, *think*," says she, putting up her
hand to stay him from further speech. "All
this is said in a moment of angry excitement; you have called me your friend, and
truly. I am so far at touch with you that
I can see you are very unhappy. You have
had—forgive me if I probe you—but you
have had some — some words with your
wife ? "

" Final words. I hope—I think."

" I do *not*, however. All this will blow
over, and——. Come, Cyril, face it ! Are
you really prepared to deliberately break the
last link that holds you to her ? "

" There is no link. She has cut herself
adrift long since. She will be *glad* to be
rid of me."

" And you ; will you be glad to be rid
of her ? "

" It will be better," says he shortly.

" And—the boy ? "

"Don't let us go into it," says he, a little wildly.

"Oh, but we must—we must," says she. "The boy—you will——"

"I shall leave him to her. It is all she has. I am nothing to her. I cannot leave her desolate."

"How you consider her," says she, in a choking voice. She could have burst into tears. What a heart! and that woman to treat him so, whilst—— Oh, it is hard, *hard!*

"I tell you," says she presently, "that you have not gone into this thing. To-morrow you will regret all that you have now said."

"If you refuse me—yes. It lies in your hands, now. *Are* you going to refuse me?"

"Give me a moment," says she, faintly. She has risen to her feet, and is so standing that he cannot watch her. Her whole soul is convulsed. Shall she? Shall she not? The scales are trembling.

That woman's face? How it rises before

her now; pale, cold, contemptuous. With
what an insolent air she had almost ordered
her from her sight. And yet—and yet——

She can remember that disdainful face kind,
and tender, and loving! A face she had
once delighted to dwell upon! And Isabel
had been very good to her once—when others
had not been kind—and when Swansdown,
her natural protector, had been scandalously
untrue to his trust. Isabel had loved her
then, and now, how was she about to requite
her? Was she to let her *know* her to be false,
not only in thought but in reality? Could
she live and see that pale face, in imagina-
tion, filled with scorn for the desecrated
friendship that once had been a real bond
between them?

Oh! A groan that is almost a sob breaks
from her. The scale has gone down to one
side. It is all over; hope, and love, and joy.
Isabel has won.

She has been leaning against the arm of
the lounge. Now she once more sinks back

upon the seat as though standing is impossible to her.

" Well ? " says Baltimore, laying his hand gently upon hers. His touch seems to burn her. She flings his hand from her and shrinks back.

" You have decided?" says he, quickly. " You will not come with me ? "

" Oh, no, no, no ! " cries she. " It is impossible ! " A little, curious laugh breaks from her that is cruelly akin to a cry. " There is too much to remember ! " says she, suddenly.

" You think you would be wronging *her*," says Baltimore, reading her correctly. " I have told you you are at fault there. She would bless the chance that swept me out of her life. And as for me, I should have no regrets. You need not fear that."

" Ah ! That is what I *do* fear," says she, in a low tone.

" Well, you have decided," says he, after a pause. " After all, why should I feel either disappointment or surprise ? What is there about me that should tempt any woman to cast in her lot with mine ?"

" Much," says Lady Swansdown, deliberately. " But the one great essential is wanting. You have no love to give. It is all given." She leans towards him and regards him earnestly. " Do you really think you are in love with me ? Shall I tell you who you *are* in love with ? " She lets her soft cheek fall into her hand and looks up at him from under her long lashes.

" You can tell me what you will," says he, a little impatiently.

" Listen then," says she, with a rather broken attempt at gaiety. " You are in love with that good, charming, irritating, impossible, but most lovable person in the world —your own wife ! "

" Pshaw ! " says Baltimore, with an irritable gesture. " We will not discuss her, if you please."

" As you will. To discuss her or leave

her name out of it altogether will not, however, alter matters."

"You have quite made up your mind?" asks he, presently, looking at her searchingly. "You will let me go alone into exile?"

"You will not go," returns she, trying to speak with conviction, but looking very anxious.

"I certainly shall. There is nothing else left for me to do. Life here is intolerable."

"There is one thing," says she, her voice trembling. "You might make it up with her."

"Do you think I haven't tried," says he, with a harsh laugh. "I'm tired of making advances. I have done all that man can do. No; I shall not try again. My one regret in leaving England will be that I shall not see you again!"

"*Don't!*" says she, hoarsely.

"I believe, in my soul," says he, hurriedly, "that you *do* care for me. That it is only because of *her* that you will not listen to me."

"You are right. I"—in a low tone—"I——". Her voice fails her. She presses her hands tightly together. "I confess," says she, with terrible abandonment, "that I might have listened to you, had I not liked *her* so well."

"Better than me, apparently," says he, bitterly. "She has had the best of it all through."

"There we are quits then," says she, quite as bitterly. "Because you like her better than me."

"If so, do you think I would speak to you as I have spoken?"

"Yes, I think that. A man is always more or less of a baby. Years of discretion he seldom reaches. You are angry with your wife and would be revenged upon her, and your way to revenge yourself is to make a *second* woman hate you."

"A second?"

"*I* should probably hate you in six months," says she with a touch of passion. "I am not sure that I do not hate you now."

Her nerve is fast failing her. If she had had a doubt about it before, the certainty now that Baltimore's feeling for her is merely friendship—the desire of a lonely man for some sympathetic companion—*anything* but love—has entered into her and crushed her. He would devote the rest of his life to her. She is sure of that, but always it would be a life filled with an unavailing regret. A horror of the whole situation has seized upon her. She will *never* be anything more to him than a pleasant memory, whilst he to her must be an ever-growing pain. Oh, to be able to wrench herself free—to be able to forget him and blot him out of her mind for ever.

"A *second* woman!" repeats he, as if struck by this thought to the exclusion of all others.

"Yes."

" You think, then," gazing at her, " that
she hates me ? "

Lady Swansdown breaks into a low but
mirthless laugh.   The most poignant anguish
rings through it.

" She—*she !* " cries she, as if unable to con-
trol herself, and then stops suddenly, placing
her hand on her forehead.   " Oh, no, *she*
doesn't hate you," she says.   " But how you
betray yourself !   Do you wonder I laugh ?
Did ever *any* man so give himself away ?
You have been declaring to me for months
that she hates you, yet when *I* put it into
words, or you think I do, it seems as though
some fresh new evil had befallen you.   Ah,
give up this *rôle* of Don Juan, Baltimore.   It
doesn't suit you."

" I have had no desire to play the part,"
says he with a frown.

" No ?   And yet you ask a woman, for
whom you scarcely bear a passing affection,
to run away with you—to defy public opinion
for your sake, and so forth.   You would advise

her to count the world well lost for love—
such love as yours ? You pour every bit of
the old rubbish into one's ears, and yet——"
she stops abruptly. A very storm of anger
and grief and despair is shaking her to her
heart's core.

" Well ? " says he, still frowning.

" What have you to offer me in exchange
for all you ask me to give up ? A heart
filled with thoughts of another ! No
more ! . . . ."

" If you persist in thinking——"

" Why should I *not* think it ? When I
tell you there is danger of my hating you,
as your wife might perhaps hate you—your
first thought is for her ! ' You think, then,
that she hates me ? ' " (she imitates the
anxiety of his tone with angry truthfulness).
" Not one word of horror at the thought
that *I* might hate you six months hence."

" Perhaps I did not believe you would,"
says he with some embarrassment.

" Ah, that is so like a man ! You think,

don't you, that you were made to be loved. There, *go* .... leave me ...."

He would have spoken to her again, but she rejects the idea with such bitterness that he is necessarily silent. She has covered her face with her hands .... Presently she is alone.

CHAPTER X

> " But there are griefs, ay, griefs as deep :
>   The friendship turned to hate,
> And deeper still, and deeper still
>   Repentance come too late, too late ! "

JOYCE, on the whole, had not enjoyed last night's dance at the Court. Barbara had been there, and she had gone home with her and Monkton after it, and on waking this morning a sense of unreality, of dissatisfaction, is all that comes to her. No pleasant flavour is on her mental palate, there is only a vague feeling of failure and a dislike to looking into things—to analyse matters as they stand.

Yet where the failure came in she would have found it difficult to explain even to herself. Everybody, so far as she was concerned, had behaved perfectly, that is, as she— if she had been compelled to say it *out loud*—

would have desired them to behave. Mr. Beauclerk had been polite enough, not *too* polite, and Lady Baltimore had made a great deal of her, and Barbara had said she looked lovely, and Freddy had said something—oh, absurd, of course, and not worth repeating, but still flattering—and those men from the barracks at Clonbree had been a perfect nuisance, they were so pressing with their kind attentions, and so eager to get a dance, and Mr. Dysart——

Well, that fault could not be laid to *his* charge; therefore, of course, he was all that could be desired. *He* was circumspect to the last degree. *He* had not been pressing with his attentions. He had indeed been *so* kind and nice that he had only asked her for one dance, and during the short quarter of an hour that that took to get through he had been so admirably conducted as to restrain his conversation to the most commonplace, and had not suggested that the conservatory was a capital place to get cool in between the dances.

The comb—she was doing her hair at the
time—caught in her hair as she came to
this point, and she flung it angrily from
her, and assured herself that the tears that
had suddenly come into her eyes arose from
the pain that that hateful instrument of torture
had caused her.

Yes—Felix had taken the right course.
He had at last learned that she could never
be anything to him—could never forgive him.
It showed great dignity in him, great strength
of mind. She had told him—at least given
him to understand—when in London, that he
should forget her, and he *had* forgotten.
He had obeyed her. The comb must have
hurt her again, and worse *this* time, because
now the tears are running down her cheeks.
How horrible it is to be unforgiving. People
who don't forgive *never* go to Heaven. There
seems to be some sort of vicious consolation
in this thought.

In truth, Dysart's behaviour to her since
his return had been all she had led him to

understand it *ought* to be. He is so changed
towards her in every way, that sometimes
she has wondered if he has forgotten all the
strange, unhappy past, and is now entirely
emancipated from the torture of love unre-
quited that once had been his.

It is a train of thought she has up to this
shrank from pursuing, yet which (she being
strong in certain ways) should have been
pursued by her, to the bitter end. One small
fact, however, had rendered her doubtful. She
cannot fail to notice that whenever he and she
were together, in morning-room, ball-room, or
at luncheon or dinner, or breakfast, though he
will not approach or voluntarily address her,
unless she first makes an advance towards
him—a rare occurrence—still, if she raises
her eyes to his—anywhere, at any moment—
it is to find *his* on her.

And what *sad* eyes ! Searching, longing,
despairing, angry, but always full of an
indescribable tenderness.

Last night she had specially noticed this,

but then last night he had especially held aloof from her. No, no. It was no use dwelling upon it. He would not forgive. That chapter in her life was closed. To attempt to open it again would be to court defeat.

Joyce, however, had not been the only one to whom last night had been a disappointment. Beauclerk's determination to propose to her, to put his fortune to the touch, and so gain hers, failed. Either the fates were against him, or else she herself was in a wilful mood. She had refused to leave the dancing room with him on any pretext whatsoever, unless to gain the coolness of the crowded hall outside, or the still more inhabited supper-room.

He was not dismayed, however. And there was no need to do things precipitately. There was plenty of time. There could be *no* doubt about the fact that she preferred him to any of the other men of her acquaintance. He had discovered that she had refused Dysart not only once, but twice. This he had drawn out of Isabel by a mild and apparently meaningless, but nevertheless incessant and abstruse, cross-examination. Naturally! He could see at once the reason for that. No girl who had been once honoured by *his* attentions could possibly give her heart to another. No girl ever yet refused an honest offer unless her mind was filled with the image of another fellow. Mr. Beauclerk found no difficulty about placing " the other fellow ' in this case. Norman Beauclerk was *his* name ! What woman in her senses would prefer that tiresome Dysart—with his " down-right honesty " business so gloomily developed —to him—Beauclerk ? Answer : not one.

Well, she shall be rewarded now, *dear* little girl. He will make her happy for life by laying his name and—prospective—fortune at her feet ! To-day he will end his happy bachelor state, and sacrifice himself on the altar of love.

Thus resolved, he walks up through the lands of the Court through the valley filled with opening fronds of ferns, and through the spinney beyond that again, until he comes to where the Monktons live. The house seems very silent; knocking at the door, the maid comes to tell him that Mr. and Mrs. Monkton and the children are out, but that Miss Kavanagh is within.

Happy circumstance. Surely the fates favour him. They always *have*, by-the-bye, sure sign that he is deserving of good luck.

Thanks. Miss Kavanagh then. His compliments, and hopes that she is not too fatigued to receive him.

The maid having shown him into the drawing-room retires with the message, and presently the sound of little high-heeled shoes crossing the hall tells him that Joyce is approaching. His heart beats high—not immoderately high—to be uncertain is to be more or less unnerved, but there is no uncertainty about *his* wooing. Still, it pleases him to know that in spite of her fatigue she could not bring herself to deny herself to *him*.

"Ah! How *good* of you," says he as she

enters, meeting her with both hands out-stretched. "I feared the visit was too early ! A very *bêtise* on my part ! But you are the soul of kindness always."

" *Early !* " says Joyce, with a little laugh. " Why you might have found me chasing the children round the garden three hours ago. Providentially," giving him one hand, the ordinary one and ignoring his other, " their father and mother were bound to go down to Lisdown this afternoon and took them with them or I should have been dead long before this."

" Ah ! " says Beauclerk, and then with increasing tenderness. " So glad they were removed. It would have been too much for you, wouldn't it ? "

" Yes—I daresay—though on the whole I don't believe I mind them," says Miss Kavanagh. " Well, and what about last night, it was delightful, wasn't it ? "

Secretly she sighs heavily, as she makes this most untruthful assertion.

"Ah! *was* it?" asks he. "*I* did not find it so. How could I, when you were so un-kind to me."

"I—oh no. Oh, surely not!" says she anxiously. There is no touch of the coquetry that might have been about this answer had it been given to a man better liked. A slow soft colour has crept into her cheeks, born of the knowledge that she had got out of several dances with him, but he, seeing it, gives it another—a more flattering meaning to his own self-love.

"Can you deny it?" asks he, changing his seat so as to get nearer to her. "Joyce," he leans towards her, "may I speak at last? Last night I was foiled in my purpose. It is difficult to say all that is in one's heart at a public affair of that kind, but now— now——"

Miss Kavanagh has sprung to her feet.

"No. Don't, *don't!*" she says earnestly. "I tell you—I beg you. I warn you——" she pauses as if not knowing what else to say,

and raises her pretty hands as if to enforce her
words.

" Shy, delightfully shy ! " says Mr. Beauclerk to himself. He goes quickly up to her
with all the noble air of the conqueror, and
seizing one of the trembling hands holds it
in his own.

" Hear me," he says with an amused tolera-
tion of her girlish *mauvaise honte*.   " It is only
such a little thing I have to say to you, but
yet it means a great deal to *me*—and to you, I
hope.   I love you, Joyce, I have come here
to-day to ask you to be my wife."

" I *told* you not to speak," says she.   She
has grown very white now.   " I warned you.
It is no use—no use indeed."

" I have startled you," says Beauclerk, still
disbelieving, yet somehow loosening the clasp
on her hand.   " You did not expect, perhaps,
that I should . have spoken to-day, and
yet——"

" No, it was not that," says Miss Kavanagh
slowly.   " I knew you would speak — I

thought last night would have been the time, but I managed to avoid it then, and now——"

" Well ? "

" I thought it better to get it over," says she gently. She stops as if struck by something, and heavy tears rush to her eyes. Ah! she had told another very much the same as that. But she had not meant it then, and yet had been believed ; now, when she does mean it, she is not believed ! Oh, if the cases might be reversed !

Beauclerk, however, mistakes the cause of the tears.

" It — get what over ? " demands he, smiling.

" This misunderstanding."

" Ah, yes, *that*. I am afraid," he leans more closely towards her, "I have *often* been afraid that you have not quite read me as I ought to be read."

" Oh, I have read you," says she, with a little gesture of her head, half confused, half mournful.

"But not rightly, perhaps. There have been moments when I fear you may have misjudged me."

"Not one," says she quickly. "Mr. Beauclerk, if I might *implore* you not to say another word."

"Only one more," pleads he, coming up smiling as usual. "Just one. Joyce, let me say my last word ; it may make all the difference in the world between you and me now. I love you—— Nay hear me ! " she has risen, and he, rising too, takes possession of both her hands, "I have come here to-day to ask you to be my wife ; you know that already, but you do *not* know how I have worshipped you all these dreary months, and how I have kept silent—for your sake."

"And for '*my sake*,' why do you speak now ? " asks she. She has withdrawn her hands from his. "What have you to offer me now that you had not a year ago ? "

After all it is a great thing to be an accomplished liar. It sticks to Beauclerk now.

"Why! Haven't you *heard?*" asks he, lifting astonished brows.

"I have heard nothing!"

"Not of my coming appointment?"—modestly. "At least of my chance of it?"

"No. Nothing—nothing. And even if I had it would make no difference. I beg you to understand once for all, Mr. Beauclerk, that I cannot listen to you."

"Not now perhaps. I have been very sudden—but——"

"No. Never. Never!"

"Are you telling me that you refuse me?" asks he, looking at her with a rather strange expression in his eyes.

"I am sorry you put it that way," returns she faintly.

"I don't believe you know what you are doing," cries he, losing his self-control for once in his life. "You will repent this! For a moment of spite, of ill-temper, you——"

"Why should I be ill-tempered about any-

thing that concerns you and me ?" says she
—very gently still.   She has grown even
whiter, however, and has lifted her head so
that her large eyes are directed straight to
his.   Something in the calm severity of her
look chills him.

"Ah ! *you* know best," says he viciously.
The game is up—is thoroughly played out.
This he acknowledges to himself, and the
knowledge does not help to sweeten his
temper.   It helps him, however, to direct a
last shaft at her.   Taking up his hat he
makes a movement to depart, and then looks
back at her.   His overweening vanity is still
alive.

"When you *do* regret it," says he, "and I
believe that will be soon—it will be too late !
You had the goodness to give me a warning
a few minutes ago.   I give you one now."

"I   shall   not   regret   it,"   returns   she
coldly.

"Not even when Dysart has sailed for
India, and ' the girl he left behind him ' is

disconsolate ? " asks he with an insolent laugh. " Hah ! *That* touches you ! "

It *has* touched her. She looks like a living thing stricken suddenly into marble, as she stands gazing back at him, with her hands tightly clenched before her. India ! To India ! And she had never heard.

Extreme anger, however, fights with her grief, and overcoming it, enables her to answer her adversary.

" I think you too will feel regret," says she gravely. " When you look back upon your conduct to me to-day."

There is such gentleness, such dignity in her rebuke, and her beautiful face is so full of a mute reproach, that all the good there is in Beauclerk rises to the surface. He flings his hat upon a table near, and himself at her feet.

" Forgive me ! " cries he in a stifled tone. " Have mercy on me, Joyce ! I love you— I swear it ! Do not cast me adrift ! All I have said or done I regret now ! You *said* I should regret, and I do."

Something in his abasement disgusts the
girl, instead of creating pity in her breast.
She shakes herself free of him by a sharp and
horrified movement.

"You must go home," she says calmly, yet
with a frowning brow. "And you must not
come here again. I *told* you it was all
useless, but you would not listen. No—*no*—
not a word!" He has risen to his feet, and
would have advanced towards her, but she
waves him from her with a sort of troubled
hatred in her face.

"You mean——" begins he hoarsely.

"One thing—one thing only," feverishly.
"That I hope I shall *never see you
again!*"

CHAPTER XI.

WHEN he is gone Joyce draws a deep breath. For a moment it seems to her that it is all over—a disagreeable task performed ; and then suddenly a reaction sets in. The scene gone through has tried her more than she knows, and now, without warning, she finds she is crying bitterly.

How *horrible* it all had been. How detestable he had looked—not so much when offering her his hand—(as for his heart, pah !)—as when he had given way to his weak exhibition of feeling, and had knelt at her feet, throwing himself on her mercy. She places her hands over her eyes when she thinks of that. Oh ! she *wishes* he hadn't done it !

She is still crying softly—not now for
Beauclerk's unpleasant behaviour, but for
certain past beliefs—when a knock at the
door warns her that another visitor is
coming.

She has not had time or sufficient presence
of mind to tell a servant that she is not at
home, when Miss Maliphant is ushered in by
the parlour-maid.

"I thought I'd come down and have a chat
with you about last night," she begins in her
usual loud tones, and with an assumption of
easiness that is belied by the keen and searching glance she directs at Joyce.

"I'm so glad," says Joyce, telling her little
lie as bravely as she can, whilst trying to
conceal her red eyelids from Miss Maliphant's
astute gaze, by pretending to rearrange a
cushion that has fallen from one of the
lounges.

"Are you?" says her visitor drily.
"Seems to me I've come at the wrong moment. Shall I go away?"

"Go! No," says Joyce, reddening and frowning a little. "Why should you?"

"Well, you've been crying," says Miss Maliphant in her terribly downright way. "I *hate* people when *I've* been crying. But then it makes me a fright, and it only makes you a little less pretty. I suppose I mustn't ask what it is all about?"

"If you did, I don't believe I could tell you," says Joyce, laughing rather unsteadily. "I was merely thinking, and it is the simplest thing in the world to feel silly now and then."

"Thinking? Of Mr. Beauclerk?" asks Miss Maliphant promptly and without the slightest idea of hesitation. "I saw him leaving this, as I came by the upper road. Was it he who made you cry?"

"Certainly not," says Joyce indignantly.

"It looks like it, however," says the other, her masculine voice growing even sterner. "What was he saying to you?"

"I really *do* think——" Joyce is beginning

coldly, when Miss Maliphant stops her by
an imperative gesture.

"Oh, I know. I know *all* about that,"
says she, contemptuously. "One shouldn't
ask questions about other people's affairs.
I've *learned* my manners, though I seldom
make any use of my knowledge, I admit. After
all, I see no reason why I *shouldn't* ask you
that question. I want to know, and there
is no one to tell me but you. Was he
proposing to you? Eh?"

"Why should you think that?" says
Joyce, subdued by the masterful manner of
the other, and by something honest and
above-board about her that is her chief
characteristic. There is no suspicion either
about her, of her questions being prompted
by mere idle curiosity. She had said she
wanted to know, and there was meaning in
her tone.

"Why shouldn't I?" says she now.
"He comes down here early this afternoon. He goes away in haste, and I find

you in tears. Everything points the one way."

" I don't see why it should point in *that* direction."

" Come, be open with me," says the heiress brusquely, in an abrupt fashion that still fails to offend. " *Did* he propose to you ? "

Joyce hesitates. She raises her head and looks at Miss Maliphant earnestly. What a *good* face she has—if plain. Too good to be made unhappy. After all, why not tell her the truth ? It would be a warning. It is impossible to be blind to the fact that Miss Maliphant had been glad to receive the dishonest attentions paid her every now and then by Beauclerk. Those attentions would probably be increased now, and would end but one way. He would get Miss Maliphant's money, and *she*—that good, kind-hearted girl —what would *she* get ? It seems cruel to be silent, and yet to speak is difficult. Would it be fair or honourable to divulge his secret ?

Would it be fair or honourable to let *her*

imagine what is not true. He had been false
to her—Joyce (she could not hide from herself the knowledge that with all his affected
desire for her, he would never have made
her an offer of his hand, but for her having
fallen in for that money)—he would therefore be false to Miss Maliphant. He would
marry her, undoubtedly, and as a husband,
he would break her heart. Is she, for the
sake of a word or two, to see her fall a prey
to a mere passionless fortune-hunter? A
thousand times no! Better inflict a little
pain now, rather than let the girl endure
endless pain in the future.

With a shrinking at her heart, born of
the fear that the word will be very bitter to
her guest, she says:

"Yes," distinctly.

"Hah!" says Miss Maliphant, and that
is all. Joyce, regarding her anxiously, is
as relieved as astonished to see no trace
of grief or chagrin upon her face. There
is no change at all, indeed, except that she

looks deeply reflective. Her mind seems to be travelling backwards, picking up loose threads of memory, no doubt, and joining them together. A sense of intense comfort fills Joyce's soul. After all, the wound had not gone deep. She had been right to speak.

" He is not worth thinking about," says she tremulously, *àpropos* of nothing as it seems.

" No ? " says Miss Maliphant. " Then what were you crying about ? "

" I hardly know. I felt nervous, and once I *did* like him—not *very* much—but still, I liked him ; and he was a disappointment."

" Tell you what," says Miss Maliphant. " You've hit upon a big truth. He is *not* worth thinking about. Once, perhaps, I, too, liked him, and I was an idiot for my pains ; but I sha'n't like him again in a hurry. I expect I've got to let him know *that*, one way or another. And, as for you——"

"I tell you I never liked him *much*," says Joyce, with a touch of displeasure. "He was handsome, suave, agreeable, but——"

"He *was*, and *is*, a hypocrite!" interrupts Miss Maliphant, with truly beautiful conciseness. She has never learned to mince matters. "And when all is told, perhaps nothing better than a fool. You are well out of it, in my opinion."

"I don't think I had much to do with it," says Joyce, unable to refrain from a smile. "I fancy my poor uncle was responsible for the honour done me to-day." Then a sort of vague feeling that she is being ungenerous distresses her. "Perhaps, after all, I misjudge him too far," she says.

"*Could* you?" with a bitter little laugh.

"I don't know," doubtfully. "One often forms an opinion of a person, and though the ground-work of it may be just, still one is too inclined to build upon it and to rear stories upon it, that get a little beyond the actual truth when the structure is completed."

"Oh, I think it is *he* who tells all the stories," says Miss Maliphant, who is singularly dull in little unnecessary ways, and has failed to follow Joyce in her upstairs flight. "In my opinion he's a liar. I was going to say *pur et simple*, but he is neither pure nor simple."

"A liar!" says Joyce, as if shocked. Some old thought recurs to her. She turns quickly to Miss Maliphant. The thought grows into words almost before she is aware of it.

"Have you a cousin in India?" asks she.

"In India?" Miss Maliphant regards her with some surprise. Why this sudden absurd question in the middle of an interesting conversation about that "Judas." I regret to say that is what Miss Maliphant has now decided upon naming Mr. Beauclerk when talking to herself.

" Yes ; India."

" Not one. Plenty in Manchester and Birmingham, but not one in India."

Joyce leans back in her chair and a strange laugh breaks from her. She gets up suddenly, and goes to the other, and leans over her, as though the better to see her.

" Oh think, *think*," says she. " Not a cousin you loved ? *Dearly* loved ? A cousin for whom you were breaking your heart ? Who was not as steady as he ought to be, but who——"

" You must be going out of your mind," says Miss Maliphant, drawing back from her. " If you saw my Birmingham cousins, or even the Manchester ones, you wouldn't ask that question twice. They think of nothing but money, money, money, from morning till night, and are essentially shoppy. I don't mind saying it, you know. It is as good to give up and acknowledge things, and certainly they——"

" Never mind them. It is the Indian

cousin in whom I am interested," says Joyce impatiently. "You are sure, *sure* that you haven't one out there? One whom Mr. Beauclerk knew about, and who was in love with you and you with him? The cousin he told me of."

"Mr. Beauclerk?"

"Yes, yes. You remember the night of the ball at the Court, last autumn. I saw you with Mr. Beauclerk in the gardens then, and he told me afterwards, you had been confiding in him about your cousin. The one in India. That you were going to be married to him. Oh! there *must* be truth —*some* truth in it. Do *try* to think!"

"If," says Miss Maliphant slowly, "I were to think until I was black in the face—as black as any Indian of 'em all—I couldn't, even by so severe a process, conjure up a cousin in Hindostan. And so he told you that?"

"Yes," says Joyce faintly. She feels almost physically ill.

"He's positively unique!" says Miss Maliphant after a slight pause. "I told you just now that he was a liar, but I didn't throw sufficient enthusiasm into the assertion. He is a liar of distinction ; very far above his fellows. I suppose it would be superfluous now to ask if, that night you speak of, you were engaged to Mr. Dysart?"

"Oh *no*," says Joyce quickly, as if struck. "There never has been, there never *will* be anything of that sort between me and Mr. Dysart. Surely Mr. Beauclerk did not——"

"Oh, yes, he did ! He assured me—not in so many words (let me be perfectly just to him), but he positively gave me to understand that you were going to marry Felix Dysart. There, don't mind that," seeing the girl's pained face, "he was bound to say *something*, you know, though it must be confessed, the Indian cousin's story was the more ingenious. Why didn't you tell me of that before?"

" Because he told it to me in the strictest confidence."

" Of course. Bound you on your honour not to speak of it, lest my feelings should be hurt. Really, do you know, I think he was almost clever enough to make one sorry he didn't succeed. Well, good-bye." She rises abruptly, and taking Joyce's hand looks at her for a moment. " Felix Dysart has a good heart," says she suddenly. As suddenly she kisses Joyce, and crossing the room with a quick stride, leaves it.

CHAPTER XII

"Shall we not laugh, shall we not weep?"

It is quite four o'clock and therefore two hours later. Barbara has returned and has learned the secret of Joyce's pale looks and sad eyes, and is now standing on the hearthrug, looking as one might who has been suddenly wakened from a dream that had seemed only too real.

"And you mean to say—you *really* mean, Joyce, that you refused him."

"Yes. I actually had that much common sense," with a laugh that has something of bitterness in it.

"But I thought—I was sure——"

"I know. You thought he was my ideal of all things admirable. And you thought wrong."

"But if not he——"

"*Barbara!*" says Joyce sharply. "Is it not enough that you should have made *one* mistake? Must you insist on making another?"

"Well, never mind," says Mrs. Monkton hastily, "I'm glad I made *that* one at all events. And I'm only sorry you have felt it your duty to make your pretty eyes wet about it. Good gracious," looking out of the window, "who is coming now? Dicky Browne and Mr. Courtenay, and those detestable Blakes. Tommy," turning sharply to her first-born, "if you and Mabel stay here, you must be *good.* Do you hear, now, *good!* You are not to ask a single question, or touch a thing in the room, and you are to keep Mabel quiet. I am not going to have Mrs. Blake go home and say you are the worst behaved children she ever met in her life. You will stay, Joyce?" anxiously to her sister.

"Oh, I suppose so. I couldn't leave you to endure their tender mercies alone."

" That's a darling girl. You know I never *can* get on with that odious woman——! Ah! how d'ye do, Mrs. Blake? How sweet of you to come and see me to-day, after last night's fatigue."

"Well, I think a drive a capital thing after being up all night," says the new comer, a fat, little, ill-natured woman, nestling herself into the cosiest chair in the room. " I hadn't *quite* meant to come here, but I met Mr. Browne and Mr. Courtenay, so I thought we might as well join forces, and storm you in good earnest. Mr. Browne has just been telling me that Lady Swansdown left the Court this morning. Got a telegram, she said, summoning her to Gloucestershire. Never *do* believe in those sudden telegrams myself. Stayed rather long in that ante-room with Lord Baltimore last night, I fancy."

" I didn't know she had been in any ante-room," says Mrs. Monkton coldly. " I dare-say her mother-in-law is ill again. She has always been very attentive to her."

"Not on terms with her son, you know; so Lady Swansdown hopes by the attention you speak of, to come in for the old lady's private fortune. Very considerable fortune I've been told."

"Who told you?" asks Mr. Browne with a cruelly lively curiosity. "Lady Swansdown?"

"Oh, dear no!"

Pause. Dicky still looking expectant, and Mrs. Blake uncomfortable. She is raking her brain to try and find some reasonable person who *might* have told her, but her brain fails her.

The pause threatens to be ghastly, when Tommy comes unconsciously to the rescue.

He had been told off, as we know, to keep Mabel in a proper frame of mind, but, being in a militant mood, has resented the task appointed him. He has, indeed, so far given in to the powers that be, that he has consented to accept a picture-book, and to show it to Mabel, who is looking at it with him, lost in admiration of its remarkable powers of description.   Each picture, indeed, is graphically explained by Tommy at the top of his lungs, and in extreme bad humour.

He is lying on the rug on his fat stomach, and is becoming quite a martinet.

" Look at this ! " he is saying now. " *Look*, do you hear ? or I won't stay and keep you good any longer.   Here's a picture about a boat that is going to be drowned down in the sea, all in one minnit.   The name of it is," reading, laboriously, " ' All Hands to the Pump.'   And," with considerable vicious enjoyment, " it isn't a bit of good for them either.   Here," pointing at the picture again with a stout little forefinger, " here they're all ' handsing ' at the pump !   See ? "

" No, I don't, and I don't *want* to," says Mabel, whimpering, and hiding her eyes. " Oh ! I don't *like* it !   It's a *horrid* pic- ture !   What's that man down there in the corner ? " peeping through her fingers at a dead man in the foreground.   " He's dead !   I *know* he is ! "

"Of course he is," says Tommy. "And," valiantly, "I don't care a bit, I don't."

"Oh! but I do," says Mabel. "And there's a lot of water, isn't there?"

"There always is in the sea," says Tommy.

"They'll *all* be drowned, I know they will," says Mabel, pushing away the book. "Oh! I *hate* 'handsing.' Turn over, Tommy, *do!* It's a nasty, cruel, wicked picture!"

"Tommy, don't frighten Mabel," says his mother anxiously.

"I'm not frightening her. I'm only keeping her quiet," says Tommy defiantly.

"Hah, hah!" says Mr. Courtenay vacuously.

"How wonderfully unpleasant children *can* make themselves!" says Mrs. Blake, making herself "wonderfully unpleasant" on the spot. "Your little boy so reminds me of my Reginald. He pulls his sister's hair merely for the fun of hearing her squeal!"

" Tommy does not pull Mabel's hair,"
says Barbara, a little stiffly. " Tommy,
come here and talk to Mr. Browne, he
wants to speak to you."

" I want to know if you would like a
cat," says Mr. Browne, drawing Tommy on
to his knee.

" I don't want a cat like *our* cat," says
Tommy promptly. " Ours is so small, and
her tail is too thin. Lady Baltimore has
a nice cat, with a tail like mamma's furry
for her neck."

" Well, that's the very sort of cat I can
get you if you wish."

" But is the cat as big as her tail ? " asks
Tommy, still careful not to commit himself.

" Well, perhaps not quite," says Mr.
Browne gravely. " Must it be quite as big ? "

" I hate small cats," says Tommy, " I
want a big one ! I want——" pausing to
find a suitable simile, and happily remembering the kennel outside, " a regular *setter*
of a cat ! "

"Ah !" says Mr. Browne, "I expect I shall have to telegraph to India for a tiger for you."

"A real live Tiger ?" asks Tommy, with distended eyes and a flutter of wild joy at his heart, the keener that some fear is mingled with it. "A Tiger that eats people up ?"

"A man-eater," says Mr. Browne solemnly. "It would be the nearest approach I know to the animal you have described. As you won't have the cat that Lady Baltimore will give you, you must only try to put up with mine."

"*Poor* Lady Baltimore !" lisps Mrs. Blake affectedly. "What a great deal she has to endure."

"Oh ! she's all right to-day," returns Mr. Browne cheerfully. "Toothache any amount better this morning."

Mrs. Blake laughs in a little mincing way.

"How *droll* you are," says she. "Ah ! if it were only *toothache* that was the matter.

But——" silence—very effective—and a profound sigh.

"Toothache's good enough for me," says Dicky. "I should never dream of asking for more." He glances here at Joyce, and continues *sotto voce*. "*You* look as if you had got it!"

"No," returns she innocently. "*Mine* is neuralgia. A rather worse thing perhaps after all."

"Yes. You can get the tooth out," says he.

"Have you heard," asks Mrs. Blake, "that Mr. Beauclerk is going to marry that *hideous* Miss Maliphant? Horrid Manchester person, don't you know! Can't think what Lady Baltimore sees in her, except," with a giggle, "her want of beauty. Got rather too much of pretty women, I should say."

"I'm really afraid that somebody has been hoaxing you this time, Mrs. Blake," says Dicky genially. "I happen to know for a fact that Miss Maliphant is not going to marry Beauclerk."

"Indeed!" snappishly. "Ah! well really he is to be congratulated, I think. Perhaps," with a sharp glance at Joyce, "I mistook the name of the young lady; I certainly heard he was going to be married."

"So am I," says Mr. Browne, "some time or other. We are all going to get married one day or another. One day, indeed, is as good as another. You have set us such a capital example that we're eager to follow it."

Mr. and Mrs. Blake being a notoriously unhappy couple, the latter grows rather red here, and Joyce gives Dicky a reproachful glance, which he returns with one of the wildest bewilderment. What *can* she mean?

"Mr. Dysart will be a distinct loss when he goes to India," continues Mrs. Blake quickly. "Won't be back for years I hear; and leaving so soon too. A disappointment I'm told! Some obdurate fair one! Sort

of chest affection, don't you know, ha ! ha !
India's the place for that sort of thing.
Knock it out of him in no time. Thought
he looked rather down in the mouth last
night. Not up to much lately, it has struck
me. Seen much of him this time, Miss
Kavanagh ? "

" Yes. A good deal," says Joyce, who
has, however, paled perceptibly.

" Thought him rather gone to seed, eh ?
Rather the worse for wear ? "

" I think him always very agreeable,"
says Joyce icily.

A second most uncomfortable silence en-
sues. Barbara tries to get up a conversation
with Mr. Courtenay, but that person, never
very brilliant at any time, seems now stricken
with dumbness. Into this awkward abyss
Mabel plunges this time. Evidently she had
been dwelling secretly on Tommy's com-
ments on their own cat, and is full of
thought about that interesting animal.

" Our cat is going to have chickens ! "

says she, with all the air of one who is imparting exciting intelligence.

This astounding piece of natural history is received with varied emotions by the listeners. Mr. Browne, however, is unfeignedly charmed with it, and grows as enthusiastic about it as even Mabel can desire.

"You don't say so ! When ? *Where?*" demands he with breathless eagerness.

"Don't know," says Mabel seriously. "Last time 'twas in nurse's best bonnet, but," raising a sweet, angelic little face to his, "she says she'll be *blowed* if she has them there *this* time ! "

"*Mabel!*" cries her mother, crimson with mortification.

"Yes ? " asks Mabel sweetly.

But it is too much for everyone. Even Mrs. Blake gives way for once to honest mirth, and under cover of the laughter rises and takes her departure, rather glad of the excuse to get away. She carries off Mr. Courtenay in her train.

Dicky having lingered a little while to see that Mabel isn't scolded, goes too, and Barbara, with a sense of relief, turns to Joyce.

" You look so awfully tired," says she. " Why don't you go and lie down ? "

" I thought, on the contrary, I should like to go out for a walk," says Joyce indifferently. " I confess my head is aching horribly. And that woman only made me worse."

" *What* a woman ! I wonder she told so many lies. I wonder if——"

" If Mr. Dysart is going to India," supplies Joyce calmly. " Very likely. Why not ? Most men in the army go to India one time or another."

" True !" says Mrs. Monkton with a sigh. Then in a low tone, " I shall be very sorry for him."

" Why ? If he goes," coldly, " it is by his own desire only. I see nothing to be sorry about."

" Oh ! I do," says Barbara ; and then —" Well, go out, dearest. I daresay the air *will* do you good."

CHAPTER XIII.

" 'Tis with our judgments as our watches, none
Go just alike, yet each believes his own."

LORD BALTIMORE had not spoken in a mere
fit of pique when he told Lady Swansdown
of his fixed intention of putting a term to
his present life. His last interview with his
wife had quite decided him to throw up
everything, and seek forgetfulness in travel.
Inclination had pointed towards such countries
as Africa, or the Northern parts of America,
as, being a keen sportsman, he believed there
he might find an occupation that would dis-
tract his mind from the thoughts that now
jarred upon him incessantly.

His asking Lady Swansdown to accompany
him, therefore, had been a sudden determination. To go on a lengthened shooting
expedition by oneself is one thing, to go

with a woman delicately nurtured is another. Of course, had she agreed to his proposal, all his plans must necessarily have been altered—and perhaps his second feeling after her refusal to go with him was one of unmistakable relief. His proposal to her had certainly been born of pique !

The next morning found him, however, still strong in his desire for change. The desire was even so far stronger that he now burned to put it into execution—to get away to some fresh sphere of action, and deliberately set himself to obliterate from his memory all past ties and recollections.

There was too perhaps a touch of revenge that bordered upon pleasure as he thought of what his wife would say when she heard of his decision. She, who shrank so delicately from gossip of all kinds, could not fail to be distressed by news that must inevitably leave her and her private affairs open to public criticism. Though everybody was perpetually guessing about her domestic

relations with her husband, no one as a
matter of fact knew (except indeed two)
quite the real truth about them. This
would effectually open the eyes of Society
and proclaim to everybody that, though she
had refused to demand a separation, still
she had been obliged to accept it. This
would touch her ! If in no other way could
he get at her proud spirit, here, now, he
would triumph. She had been anxious to
get rid of him—in a respectable way of
course—but Death, as usual, had declined
to step in when most wanted, and now——
well ! she must accept her release in however disreputable a guise it comes.

It is just at the moment when Mrs. Blake
is holding forth on Lady Baltimore's affairs
to Mrs. Monkton that Baltimore enters the
smaller drawing-room, where he knows he
will be sure to meet his wife at this hour.

It is far into the afternoon, but still the
spring sunshine is streaming through the
windows. Lady Baltimore, in a heavy tea-

gown of pale-green plush, is sitting by the
fire reading a book—her little son upon the
hearth-rug beside her. The place is strewn
with bricks, and the boy, as his father
enters, looks up at him, and calls to him
eagerly to come and help him. At the
sound of the child's quick, glad voice, a
pang contracts Baltimore's heart. The child.
He had forgotten him.

"I can't make this castle," says Bertie,
"and mother isn't a bit of good ; hers always
fall down. Come you, and make me one."

"Not now," says Baltimore. "Not to-day.
Run away to your nurse—I want to speak
to your mother."

There is something abrupt and jerky in
his manner—something strained, and with
sufficient temper in it to make the child
cease from entreaty. The very pain Baltimore is feeling has made his manner harsher
to the child. Yet as the latter passes him
obediently, he seizes the small figure in his
arms and presses him convulsively to his

breast; then, putting him down, he points silently but peremptorily to the door.

"Well?" says Lady Baltimore. She has risen—startled by his abrupt entrance, his tone, and more than all by that last brief but passionate burst of affection towards the child. "You wish to speak to me—*again?*"

"There won't be many more opportunities," says he grimly; "you may safely give me a few moments to-day. I bring you good news. I am going abroad. At once. For ever."

In spite of the terrible self-control she has taught herself, Lady Baltimore's self-possession gives way. Her brain seems to reel. Instinctively she grasps hold of the back of the tall *prie-Dieu* next to her.

"Hah! I thought so. I have touched her at last—through her pride," thinks Baltimore, watching her with a savage satisfaction that yet, however, hurts him horribly. And after all he was wrong too. He had touched her indeed; but it was her heart, not her pride he had wounded.

"Abroad!" echoes she faintly.

"Yes. Why not? I am sick of this sort of life. I have decided on flinging it up."

"Since when have you come to this decision?" asks she presently, having conquered her sudden weakness by a supreme effort.

"If you want day and date, I'm afraid I sha'n't be able to supply you. It has been growing upon me for some time—the idea of it, I mean; and last night—*you* brought it to perfection."

"*I?*"

"Have you already forgotten all the complimentary speeches you made me? They," with a sardonic smile, "are so sweet to me that I shall keep them ripe in my memory until death overtakes me—and *after* it, I think! You told me amongst many other wifely things—if my mind does not deceive me—that you wished me well out of your life, and Lady Swansdown with me."

"That is a direct and most malicious misapplication of my words," says she emphatically.

"Is it? I confess that was *my* reading of them. I accepted that version, and thinking to do you a good turn and relieve you of both your *bêtes noires* at once, I proposed to Lady Swansdown last night that she should accompany me upon my endless travels!"

There is a long, long pause, during which Lady Baltimore's face seems to have grown into marble. She takes a step forward now. Through the stern pallor of her skin her large eyes seem to gleam like fire.

"How dare you?" she says in a voice very low, but so intense that it rings through the room. "How *dare* you tell me of this? Are you lost to *all* shame? You and she to go—to go away together; it is only what I have been anticipating for months. I could see how it was with you! But that you should have the insolence to stand before me," she grows almost magnificent in her wrath, "and *declare* your infamy aloud—

such a thought was beyond me. There was a time when I would have thought it beyond even *you!*"

" *Was* there ? " says he.

He laughs aloud.

" There, there, there ! " says she, with a rather wild sort of sigh. " Why should I waste a single emotion upon you ? Let me take you calmly, casually. Come, come now ! " It is the saddest thing in the world to see how she treads down the passionate—most natural—uprisings within her against the in-justice of life. " Make me at least *au courant* with your movements ; you and she will go —where ?"

" To the Devil ! you hope, don't you ? " says he. " Well, you will be disappointed so far as *she* is concerned. Wherever I may be going, it appears she doesn't think it worth her while to accompany me there or anywhere else."

" You mean—that she—refused to go with you ?"

"In the very baldest language, I assure you ; it left nothing to be desired, believe me, in the matter of lucidity. No, she would not go with me ; you see, there is not only one, but *two* women in the world who regard me as being utterly without charm."

"I commiserate you," says she with a bitter sneer. "If, after all your attention to her, your friend has proved faithless, I——"

"Don't waste your pity," says he, interrupting her rather rudely. "On the whole, the decision of 'my friend,' as you call her, was rather a relief to me than otherwise. I felt it my duty to deprive *you* of her society"—with an unpleasant laugh—"and so I asked her to come with me. When she declined to accompany me, she left me free to devote myself to sport."

"Ah ! you refuse to be comforted !" says she, contemptuously.

"Think what you will," says he, restraining himself with determination. "It doesn't matter in the least to me now . . . .

your opinion I consider worthless—because prejudiced—as worthless as you consider me. I came here simply to tell you of my determination to go abroad."

"You have told me of that already. Lady Swansdown having failed you, may I ask "— with studied contempt—"who you are going to take with you *now?*"

"What do you mean?" says he, wheeling round to her. "What do you mean by that? By Heavens!" laying his hands upon her shoulders, and looking with fierce eyes into her pale face, "a man might well *kill* you!"

"And why?" demands she, undaunted. "You would have taken *her*—you have confessed so much—you had the coarse courage to put it into words—if not her, why "—with a shrug—"then another!"

"There! think as you will," says he, releasing her roughly. "*Nothing* I could say would convince or move you. And yet—I know it is no use, but I am determined I will leave nothing unsaid. I will give you no

loophole. I asked her to go with me in a
moment of irritation—of loneliness, if you will.
It is hard for a man to be for ever outside the
pale of affection, and I thought—well, it is no
matter *what* I thought. I was wrong, it
seems. As for caring for her, I care so little
that now I feel actually *glad* she had the sense
to refuse my senseless proposal. She would
have bored me, I think, and I should
undoubtedly have bored *her*. The proposi-
tion was made to her in a moment of
folly !"

"Oh, *folly !*" says she, with a curious laugh.

"Well, give it any other name you like. And,
after all "—in a low tone—" you are right.
It was *not* the word. If I had said *despair* I
should have been nearer the mark."

"There might even be another word," says
she, slowly.

"Even if there were," says he, "the
occasion for it is of your making. You have
thrown me over. You must be prepared,
therefore, to accept the consequences."

" You have prepared me for anything," says she, calmly, but with bitter meaning.

" See here," says he, furiously. " There may still be one thing left for which I have *not* prepared you. You have asked me who I am going to take with me when I leave this place for ever. Shall I answer you ?"

Something in his manner terrifies her. She feels her face blanching. Words are denied her, but she makes a faint movement of assent with her hand.

What is he going to say ?

" What if I should decide, then, on taking *my son* with me ?" says he, violently. " Who is there to prevent me ? Not you, or another. Thus I could cut *all* ties, and put you out of my life at once and for ever."

He had certainly not calculated on the force of his words—his manner. It had been a mere angry suggestion. There was no cruelty in Baltimore's nature. He had never once permitted himself to dwell upon the possibility of separating the boy from his mother. Such terrible revenge as that was beyond him. His whole nature would have revolted from it. He had spoken with passion—urged by her contempt into a desire to show her where his power lay—without any intention of actually using it. He meant, perhaps, to weaken her intolerable defiance, and show her where a hole in her armour lay. He was not prepared for the effect of his words.

An ashen shade has overspread her face. Her expression has become ghastly. As though her limbs have suddenly given way under her, she falls against the mantelpiece and clings to it with trembling fingers. Her eyes, wild and anguished, seek his.

"The child!" gasps she, in a voice of mortal terror. "The child! Not the child! Oh, Baltimore, you have taken *all* from me except that! *Leave* me my child!"

"Good Heavens! Don't look at me like that!" exclaims he, inexpressibly shocked. This sudden and complete abandonment of her to her fear has horrified him. "I never meant it ; I but suggested a possibility. The child shall stay with you—do you hear me, Isabel ? The child is *yours!* When I go, I go alone !"

There is a moment's silence, and then she bursts into tears. It is a sharp reaction, and it shakes her bodily and mentally. A wild return of her love for him shakes her—(that first sweet and only love of her life)—born of intense gratitude. But sadly, slowly, it dies away again. It seems to her too late to dream of *that* again. Yet, perhaps, her tears have as much to do with that lost love as with her gratitude.

Slowly her colour returns. She checks her sobs. She raises her head and looks at him still with her handkerchief pressed to her tremulous lips.

"It is a promise ? " says she.

" Yes, a promise."

" You will not change again ? "—nervously —" you——"

" Ah ! doubt to the last," says he. " It is a

promise from me to you ; and, of course, the word of such a reprobate as you consider me can scarcely be of any avail."

"But—you *could* not break this promise ?" says she, in a low voice, and with a long, *long* sigh.

"What *trust* you place in me !" says he, with an open sneer. "Well, so be it. I give you home and child. You give me ——. Not worth while going into the magnificence of *your* gifts, is it ?"

"I gave you once a whole heart—an unbroken faith," says she.

"And took them back again !—Child's play," says he. "Child's promises. Well, if you will have it so, you have got a promise from me now, and I think you might say 'thank you' for it, as the children do."

"I *do* thank you," says she vehemently. "Does not my whole manner speak for me ?" Once again her eyes fill with tears.

"*So* much love for the child !" cries he in a stinging tone, "and not one thought for the father. Truly your professions of love were light as thistledown. There, you are not worth a thought yourself! Expend any affection you have upon your son, and forget me as soon as ever you can. It will not take you long, once I am out of your sight."

He strides towards the door and then looks back at her.

" You understand about my going," he says. " That it is decided, I mean ? "

" As you will," says she, her glance on the ground. There is such a total lack of emotion in her whole air that it might suggest itself to an acute student of human nature that she does her very utmost to suppress even the smallest sign of it. But alas, Baltimore is not that student.

" Be just," says he sternly. " It is as *you* will, not as I. It is you who are driving me into exile."

He has turned his back and has his hand on the handle of the door in the act of opening it. At this instant she makes a movement towards him, holding out her hands, but as suddenly suppresses herself. When he turns again to say a last word, she is standing where he last saw her, pale and impassive as a statue.

"There will be some matters to arrange," says he, "before my going. I have telegraphed to Hansard" (his lawyer); "he will be down in the morning. There will be a few papers for you to sign to-morrow——"

"Papers!"

"My will and your maintenance whilst I am away, and matters that will concern the child's future."

"His future! That means——"

"That in all probability when I have started I shall never see his face again—or yours."

He opens the door abruptly and is gone.

CHAPTER XIV

"While bloomed the magic flowers we scarcely knew
  The gold was there. But now their petals strew
  Life's pathway."

.   .   .   .

"And yet the flowers were fair
  Fed by youth's dew and love's enchanted air."

THE cool evening air beating on Joyce's flushed cheeks calms her as she sets out for the walk that Barbara had encouraged her to take. It is an evening of great beauty. Earth, sea and sky seem blended in one great soft mist that, rising from the ocean down below, floats up to Heaven, its heart a pale, vague pink.

The day is almost done, and already shadows are growing round trees and corners. There is something mystical and strange in the deep murmurs that come from the nesting woods. The wild sweet coo of the pigeons, the chirping of innumerable songsters, and now and then the dull hooting of some blinking owl. Through all, the sad tolling of a chapel bell, away, away in the distance, where the tiny village hangs over the brow of the rocks that gird the sea.

> " While yet the woods were hardly more than brown,
> 　Filled with the stillness of the dying day,
> 　　The folds, and farms, and faint green pastures lay
> 　And bells chimed softly from the grey-walled town.
> 　The dark fields with the corn and poppies sown,
> 　　The dark, delicious dreamy forest way,
> 　　The hope of April for the soul of May,
> 　On all of these night's wide soft wings swept down."

Well, it isn't night yet, however. She can see to tread her way among the short young grasses down to a favourite nook of hers, where musical sounds of running streams may be heard, and the rustlings of growing leaves make songs above one's head. Here and there she goes through brambly ways, where amorous arms from blackberry bushes strive to catch and hold her, and where star-eyed daisies and butter-

cups, and delicate faint-hearted primroses,
peep out to laugh at her discomfiture. But
she escapes from all their snares, and goes
on her way, her heart so full of troublous
fancies that their many wiles gain from her
not so much as one passing thought.

The pretty, lovely May is just bursting
into bloom. Its pink blossoms here, and
its white blossoms there, mingle gloriously,
and the perfume of it fills the silent air.

Joyce picks a branch or two as she goes
on her way, and thrusts them into the
bosom of her gown.

And now she has reached the outskirts of
the wood, where the river runs, crossed by
a rustic bridge, on which she has ever loved
to rest and dream, leaning rounded arms
upon the wooden railings, and seeing strange,
but sweet things in the bright hurrying
water beneath her eyes.

She has gained the bridge, and leaning
languidly upon its frail ramparts, lets her
gaze wander afield. The little stream, full

of conversation as ever, flows on unnoticed by her. Its charm seems dead. *That* belonged to the old life, the life she will never know again. It seems to her quite a long time since she felt *young*, and yet only a few short months have flown since she was young as the best of them, when even Tommy did not seem altogether despicable as a companion, and she had often been guilty of finding pleasure in running a race with him, and covering him, not only with confusion, but armfuls of scented hay when at last she had gained the victory over him, and had turned from the appointed goal to overwhelm the enemy with merry sarcasms.

Oh, yes, that was all over—all done. An end must come to everything, and to her lightheartedness an end had come very soon. *Too* soon, she was inclined to believe in an access of self-pity, until she remembered that life was always to be taken seriously, and that she had deliberately trifled with it, seeking only the very heart of it—the gaiety, the carelessness, the ease.

Well, her punishment has come. She has learned that life is a failure after all. It takes some people a lifetime to discover that great fact, it has taken her quite a short time. Nothing is of much consequence, and yet——

She sighs and looks round her. Her eyes fall upon a distant bank of cloud overhanging a pretty farmstead, and throwing into bold relief the big rick of hay that stands at the western side of it. A huge black crow standing on the top of this, is flapping his wings and calling loudly to his mate. Presently he spreads his wings, and with a creaking of them like the noise of a sail in a light wind, disappears over her head. She has followed his movements with a sort of lazy curiosity, and now she knows that he will return in an hour or so with thousands of his brethren, darkening the heavens as they pass to their night's lodging in the tall elm trees.

It is good to be a bird. No care, no trouble, no *pain!* A short life and a merry one. Better than a long life and a sorry one. Yes, the world is all sorrow.

She turns her eyes impatiently away from the fast-vanishing crow, and now they fall upon a perfect wilderness of daffodils that are growing on the edge of the bank a little way down. How beautiful they are ! Their soft, delicate heads nod lazily this way and that. They seem the very embodiment of graceful drowsiness. Some lines, lately read, recur to her, and awake within her memory.

> " I wandered lonely as a cloud,
>   That floats on high o'er vales and hills,
>   When all at once I saw a crowd,
>   A crowd of golden daffodils,
>   Beside the lake, beneath the trees,
>   Fluttering and dancing in the breeze."

They seem so full of lazy joy, of unutterable rapture, that they belie her belief in the falseness of all things. There must

surely be some good in a world that grows
such charming things—things almost sen-
tient. And the trees swaying above her
head, and dropping their branches into the
stream, is there no delight to be got out
of *them?* The tenderness of this soft, sweet
wood in which perpetual twilight reigns,
enters into her and soothes the sad demon
that is torturing her breast. Tears rise to
her eyes : she leans still farther over the
parapet, and drawing the pink and white
hawthorn blossoms from her bosom, drops
them one by one into the hasty little river,
and lets it bear them away upon its bosom
to tiny bays unknown. Tears follow them,
falling from her drooping lids. Can neither
daffodils, nor birds, nor trees, give her some
little of their joy to chase this sorrow from
her heart ?

Her soul seems to fling itself outward in
an appeal to Nature, and Nature, that kind
mother of us all, responds to the unspoken
cry.

A step upon the bridge behind her !
She starts into a more upright position,
and looks round her without much interest.

A dark figure is advancing towards her.
Through the growing twilight it seems ab-
normally large and black, and Joyce stares
at it anxiously. Not Freddy, not one of
the labourers ; *they*—the latter—would be
all clad in flannel jackets of a light
colour.

"Oh ! is it *you ?* " says Dysart, coming
closer to her. He had, however, known it
was she from the first moment his eyes
rested on her. No mist, no twilight, could
have deceived him, for

> " Lovers' eyes are sharp to see,
> And lovers' ears in hearing."

"Yes," says she, advancing a little towards him and giving him her hand. A
cold little hand, and reluctant.

"I was coming down to Mrs. Monkton
with a message—a letter—from Lady Baltimore."

"This is a very long way round from the Court, isn't it?" says she.

"Yes; but I like this calm little corner. I have come often to it, lately."

Miss Kavanagh lets her eyes wander to the stream down below. To *this* little spot, of all places! Her favourite nook! Had he hoped to meet her there? Oh *no;* impossible! And, besides, she has given it up for a long, long time, until this evening. It seems weeks to her now since last she was here.

"You will find Barbara at home," says she, gently.

"I don't suppose it is of very much consequence," returns he, alluding to the message. He is looking at her, though her averted face leaves him little to study.

"You are cold," says he, abruptly.

"Am I?" turning to him with a little smile. "I don't *feel* cold. I feel dull, perhaps, but nothing else."

And, in truth, if she had substituted the

word unhappy for dull, she would have been nearer the mark. The coming of Dysart thus suddenly into the midst of her mournful reverie has but served to accentuate the reality of it. A terrific sense of *loneliness* is oppressing her. All things have their place in this world, yet where is *hers?* Of what account is she to anyone? Barbara loves her; yes, but not so well as Freddy or the children. Oh, to be *first* with someone!

> "I find no Spring, while Spring is well-nigh blown;
> I find no nest, while nests are in the grove;
> Woe's me for mine own heart that dwells alone,
> My heart that breaketh for a little love."

Christina Rosetti's mournful words seem to suit her. Involuntarily she lifts her heavy eyes, tired by the day's weeping, and looks at Dysart.

"You have been crying," says he abruptly.

CHAPTER XV.

" My love has sworn with sealing kiss
With me to live—to die;
I have at last my nameless bliss,
As I love—loved am I."

THERE is a pause. It threatens to be an everlasting one, as Miss Kavanagh plainly doesn't know what to say. He can see this. What he cannot see is that she is afraid of her own voice. Those troublesome tears that all day have been so close to her, seem closer than ever now.

"Beauclerk came down to see you to-day," says he, presently. This remark is so unexpected that it steadies her.

"Yes," she says, calmly enough, but without raising the tell-tale eyes.

"You expected him?"

"No." Monosyllables alone seem possible to her; so great is her fear that she will

give way and finally disgrace herself, that
she forgets to resent the magisterial tone
he has adopted.

"He asked you to marry him, however?"
There is something almost threatening in
his tone now, as if he is defying her to
deny his assertion. It overwhelms her.

"Yes," she says again, and for the first
time is struck by the wretched meagreness
of her replies.

"Well?" says Dysart, roughly. But this
time not even the desolate monosyllable
rewards the keenness of his examination.
"Well?" says he again, going closer to
her, and resting his hand on the wooden
rail against which she too is leaning. He
is so close to her now, that it is impossible
to escape his scrutiny. "What am I to
understand by that? Tell me how you
have decided." Getting no answer to this,
either, he says impatiently, "Tell me,
Joyce."

"I refused him," says she at last, in a

low tone, and in a dull sort of way, as if the matter is one of indifference to her.

"*Ah!*" He draws a long breath. "It is true?" he says, laying his hand on hers as it lies on the top of the woodwork.

"Quite so."

"And yet—you have been crying?"

"You can see that," says she petulantly. "You have taken *pains* to see, and to tell me of it. Do you think it is a pleasant thing to be told? *Most* people," glancing angrily towards him—"*everyone*, I think, makes it a point now-a-days, *not* to see when one has been making a fool of oneself, but *you* seem to take a delight in torturing me."

"Did it," says he bitterly, ignoring, perhaps not even hearing, her outburst. "Did it cost you so much to refuse him?"

"It cost me nothing!" with a sudden effort, and a flash from her beautiful eyes.

"Nothing?"

"I have said so. Nothing at all. It

was mere nervousness, and because it re-
minded me of other things."

"Did he *see* you cry?" asks Dysart,
tightening unconsciously his grasp upon her
hand.

"No. He was gone a long time—*quite* a
long time before it occurred to me that I
should like to cry. I," with a frugal smile,
"indulged myself very freely then, as you
have seen."

Dysart draws a long breath of relief. It
would have been intolerable to him that
Beauclerk should have known of her tears.
He would not have understood them. He
would have taken possession of them as it
were. They would have merely helped to
pamper his self-conceit, and smooth down
his ruffled pride. He would inevitably have
placed such and such a construction on
them—one entirely to his own glorifica-
tion.

"I shall leave you now with a lighter
heart," says Felix presently. "Now that

I know you are not going to marry that fellow."

"You *are* going, then," says she sharply, checking the monotonous little tattoo she has been playing on the bridge rail as though suddenly smitten into stone. She had heard he was going ; she had been told of it by several people, but somehow she had not believed it. It had never come home to her until now.

"Yes. We are under orders for India ; we sail in about a month. I shall have to leave here almost immediately."

"So soon," says she vaguely. She has begun that absurd tattoo again, but bridge, and restless little fingers, and sky and earth, and all things seem blotted out. He is going. *Really* going ; and for ever ! How far is India away ?

"It is always rather hurried at last. For my part I am glad I'm going."

"Yes ?"

"Mrs. Monkton will—at least I am sure

she will—let me have a line now and then
to let me know how you—how you are all
getting on. I was going to ask her about
it this evening. You think she will be good
enough ? "

" Barbara is always kind."

" I suppose——" he hesitates, and then
goes on with an effort. " I suppose it
would be too much to ask of you——"

" What ? "

" That you would sometimes write me a
letter—however short."

" I am a bad correspondent," says she,
feeling as if she is choking.

" Ah ! I see. I should not have asked,
of course. Yes, you are right. It was
absurd my hoping for it."

" When people choose to go away so far
as that——" she is compelling herself to
speak, but her voice sounds to herself a
long way off.

" They must hope for nothing better than
to be forgotten. ' Out of sight, out of mind,'

I know—it is such an *old* proverb. Well
. . . . You are cold," says he, suddenly,
noting the pallor of the girl's face. " Whatever you were before, you are certainly
chilled to the bone now. You *look* it. Come !
This is no time of year to be lingering out
of doors without a coat or hat."

" I have this shawl," says she, pointing
to the soft, white fleecy thing that covers
her.

" I distrust it. Come."

" No," says she faintly. " Go on you.
Give your message to Barbara. As for me,
I shall be happier here."

" Where I am not," says he with a bitter
laugh. "I suppose I ought to be accustomed
to that thought now, but such is my con-
ceit that it seems ever a fresh shock to me.
Well, for all that," persuasively, " come in.
The evening is very cold. I sha'n't like to
go away leaving you behind me suffering
from a bad cough or something of that kind.
We *have* been friends, Joyce," with a rather

sorry smile. "For the sake of the old friendship, don't send me adrift with such an anxiety upon my mind."

"Would you really care?" says she.

"Ah! that is the humour of it," says he. "In spite of all, I should still really care! —come." He makes an effort to unclasp the small pretty fingers that are grasping the rails so rigidly. At first they seem to resist his gentle pressure, and then they give way to him. She turns suddenly.

"Felix!" her voice is somewhat strained, somewhat harsh; not at all her own voice. "Do you still love me?"

"You know that," returns he sadly. If he has felt any surprise at the question, he has not shown it.

"No, no," says she feverishly. "That you *like* me, that you are fond of me, per-haps, I can still believe. But is it the same with you that it used to be? Do you," with a little sob, "*love* me as well now as in those old days? *Just* the same?

Not," going nearer to him and laying her hand upon his breast, and raising agonized eyes of enquiry to his, "not one bit less?"

"I love you a thousand times more," says he, very quietly, but with such intensity that it enters into her very soul. "Why?" He has laid his own hand over the small nervous one lying on his breast, and his face has grown very white.

"Because—*I love you too!*"

She stops short here and begins to tremble violently. With a little, shamed, heart-broken gesture she tears her hand out of his, and covers her face from his sight.

"Say that again," says he, hoarsely. He waits a moment, but when no word comes from her, he deliberately drags away the sheltering hands and compels her to look at him.

"*Say it*," says he, in a tone that now is almost a command.

"Oh! it is true—*true!*" cries she vehemently. "I love you. I have loved you

a long time I think, but I didn't know it.
Oh, Felix ! Dear, *dear* Felix, forgive me ! "

" *Forgive* you ? " says he brokenly.

" Ah, yes. And don't leave me. If you
go away from me I shall die ! There has
been so *much* of it—a little more, and
——" She breaks down.

" My beloved," says he in a faint, quick
way. He is holding her to him now with
all his might. She can feel the quick pulsa-
tions of his heart. Suddenly she slips her
soft arms around his neck, and now with
her head pressed against his shoulder, bursts
into a storm of tears. It is a last shower.

They are both silent for a long time, and
then he, raising one of her hands, presses the
palm against his lips. Looking up at him,
she smiles, uncertainly but happily, a very
rainbow of a smile born of sunshine and rain-
drops gone. It seems to beautify her lips.
But Felix, whilst acknowledging its charm
cannot smile back at her. It is all too
strange, too new. He is *afraid* to believe.

As yet there is something terrible to him in the happiness that has fallen into his life.

"You mean it?" he asks, bending over her. "If to-morrow I were to wake and find all this an idle dream, how would it be with me then? *Say* you mean it."

"Am I not here?" says she tremulously, making a slight but eloquent pressure on one of the arms that are round her. He bends his face to hers, and as he feels that first glad, eager, kiss returned—he *knows!*

CHAPTER XVI.

OF course Barbara is delighted. She proves charming as a confidante. Nothing can exceed the depth of her sympathy.

When Joyce and Felix come in together in the darkening twilight, entering the house in a burglarious fashion through the dining-room window, it so happens that Barbara is there, and is at once struck by a sense of guilt that seems to surround and envelop them. They had not indeed anticipated meeting Barbara in that room of all others, and are rather taken aback when they come face to face with her.

"I assure you we have not come after the spoons," says Felix in a would-be careless tone that could not have deceived an infant, and with a laugh so *frightfully* careless that it would have terrified the life out of you.

"You certainly don't look *like* it," says Mrs. Monkton whose heart has begun to beat high with hope. She hardly knows whether it is better to fall upon their necks forthwith and declare she knows all about it, or else to pretend ignorance. She decides upon the latter as being the easier. After all they mightn't like the neck process, most people have a fancy for telling their own tales. To have them told for one is annoying. "You haven't the requisite murderous expression," she says, unable to resist a touch of satire. "You look rather frightened you two. What have you been doing?" She is too good-natured not to give them an opening for their confession.

"Not much, and yet a great deal," says Felix ; he has advanced a little, whilst Joyce, on the contrary, has meanly receded farther into the background. She has rather the appearance indeed of one who, if the wall *could* have been induced to give way, would gladly have followed it into the garden. The wall, however, declines to budge. " As for burglary," goes on Felix, trying to be gay, and succeeding villainously, " you must exonerate your sister at all events. But I—I confess I have stolen something belonging to you."

" Oh, no, not *stolen*," says Joyce, in a rather faint tone. " Barbara, I know what you will think—but——"

" I know what I *do* think ! " cries Barbara, joyously. " Oh ! *is* it, *can* it be true ? "

It never occurs to her that Felix now is not altogether a brilliant match for a sister with a fortune. She remembers only in that lovely mind of hers, that he had loved Joyce when she was without a penny, and that he is now what he had always seemed to her, the one man who could make Joyce happy.

" Yes. It is true," says Dysart. He has given up that unsuccessful gaiety now, and has grown very grave. There is even a slight tremble in his voice. He comes up to Mrs. Monkton and takes both her hands. " She has given herself to me. You are *really* glad ? You are not angry about it ? I know I am not good enough for her, but——"

Here Joyce gives way to a little outburst of mirth that is rather tremulous, and coming away from the unfriendly wall that has not been of the least use to her, brings herself somewhat shamefacedly into the only light the room receives through the western window. The twilight at all events is kind to her. It is difficult to see her face.

" I really can't stay here," says she, " and listen to my own praises being sung. And besides," turning to Felix a lovely, but embarrassed face, " Barbara will not regard it as you do. She will, on the contrary, say you are a great deal too good for me, and that I ought to be pilloried for all the trouble

I have given you through not being able to make up my own mind for so long a time."

"Indeed I shall say nothing but that you are the dearest girl in the world, and that I'm delighted things have turned out so well. I always *said* it would be like this!" cries Barbara exultantly, who certainly never *had* said it, and had always indeed been distinctly doubtful about it.

"Is Mr. Monkton in?" asks Felix, in a way that leads Monkton's wife to imagine that if she should chance to say he was out, the news would be hailed with rapture.

"Oh, never mind *him*," says she, beaming upon the happy but awkward couple before her. "*I'll* tell him all about it. He will be just as glad as I am. There, go away you two; you will find the small parlour empty, and I daresay you have a great deal to say to each other still. Of course you will dine with us, Felix, and give Freddy an opportunity of saying something ridiculous to you."

"Thank you," says Dysart warmly. "I

suppose I can write a line to my cousin explaining matters."

"Of course. Joyce, take some writing things into the small parlour, and call for a lamp as you go."

She is smiling at Joyce as she speaks, and now, going up to her, kisses her impulsively. Joyce returns the caress with fervour. It is natural that she should never have felt the sweetness, the *comfort* of Barbara, so entirely as she does now, when her heart is open, and full of ecstasy, and when sympathy seems so necessary. *Darling* Barbara ! But then she must love Felix now just as much as she loves her. She rather electrifies Barbara and Felix by saying anxiously to the former :

"Kiss Felix too ! "

It is impossible not to laugh ! Mrs. Monkton gives way to immediate and un- restrained mirth, and Dysart follows suit.

"It is a command," says he, and Barbara thereupon kisses him affectionately.

" Well, now I have got a brother at last,"
says she. It is indeed her first knowledge
of one, for that poor suicide in Nice had never
been anything to her—or to anyone else in
the world for the matter of that—except a
great trouble. " There, go ! " says she. " I
think I hear Freddy coming."

They fly. They both feel that further
explanations are beyond them just at present,
and as for Barbara, she is quite determined
that no one but she shall let Freddy into
the all-important secret.

She is now fully convinced in her own
mind that she had always had special pre-
science of this affair ; and the devouring
desire we all have to say " *I* told you how
'twould be," to our unfortunate fellow-travel-
lers through this vale of tears, whether the
cause for the hateful reminder be for weal
or woe, is strong upon her.

She goes to the window, and seeing
Monkton some way off, flings up the sash,
and waves to him in a frenzied fashion to

come to her *at once.* There is something that almost approaches tragedy in her air and gesture. Monkton hastens to obey it.

"Now—what—what—*what* do you think has happened ? " cries she, when he has vaulted the window-sill and is standing beside her somewhat breathless and distinctly uneasy. Nothing short of an accident to the children could in *his* opinion have warranted so vehement a call. Yet Barbara, as he examines her features carefully, seems all joyous excitement. After a short contemplation of her beaming face, he tells himself he was an ass to give up that pilgrimage of his to the lower field, where he had been going to inspect a new-born calf.

"The skies are all right," says he, with an upward glance at them through the window. "And—you hadn't *another* uncle, had you ? "

"Oh ! Freddy," said she, very justly disgusted.

"Well, my good child, *what* then ? I'm all curiosity."

" Guess," says she, too happy to be able to give him the round scolding he deserves.

" Oh ! If it's a riddle," says he, " you might remember I am only a little one, and unequal to the great things of life ! "

" Ah ! but Freddy, I've something delicious to tell you. There, sit down there—you look quite queer—whilst I——"

" No wonder I do," says he at last, rather wrathfully. " To judge by your wild gesticulations at the window just now, anyone might have imagined that the house was on fire, and a hostile race tearing *en masse* into the backyard ! And now ! Why it appears you are quite *pleased* about something or other ! Really such disappointments are enough to age a man—or make him look ' queer.' That was the word you used, I think ? "

" Listen ! " says she, seating herself beside him, and slipping her arm round his neck. " Joyce is going to marry Felix—*after all !*

There !" Still with her arm holding him, she leans back a little to mark the effect of this astonishing disclosure.

CHAPTER XVII.

"Well said; that was laid on with a trowel."

.　　　.　　　.　　　.　　　.

"Gratiano speaks an infinite deal of nothing, more than any man in all Venice."

"AFTER all, indeed. You may well say that," says Mr. Monkton with indignation. "If those two idiots meant matrimony all along, why on earth didn't they do it before? See what a lot of time they've lost, and what a disgraceful amount of trouble they have given all round."

"Yes. Yes, of course. But then you see, Freddy, it takes some time to make up one's mind about such an important matter as that."

"It didn't take *you* long," says Mr. Monkton most unwisely.

"It took me a great deal longer than it

took you," replies his wife with dignity. "You have always said that it was the very first day you ever saw me—and I'm sure it took me quite a week."

This lucid speech she delivers with some severity.

"More shame for you," says Monkton promptly.

"Well, never mind," says she, too happy and too engrossed with her news to enjoy even a skirmish with her husband. "Isn't it all charming, Freddy?"

"It has certainly turned out very well, all things considered."

"I think it is the happiest thing. And when two people who love each other are *quite* young——"

"Really, my dear, you are too flattering," says Monkton. "Considering the grey hairs that are beginning to make themselves so unpleasantly at home in my head, I, at all events, can hardly lay claim to extreme youth."

" Good gracious ! I'm not talking of *us*,
I'm talking of *them*," cries she, giving him
a shake. " Wake up, Freddy. Bring your
mind to bear upon this big news of mine,
and you will see how enchanting it is. *Don't*
you think Felix has behaved beautifully, so
faithful—*so* constant—and against such terrible odds. You know, Joyce *is* a little
difficult sometimes ! Now *hasn't* he been
perfect all through ? "

" He is a genuine Hero of Romance," says
Mr. Monkton with conviction. "None of
your cheap articles — a regular bonâ-fide
thirteenth-century knight. The country
ought to contribute its stray halfpennies
and buy him a pedestal and put him on
the top of it, whether he likes it or not.
Once there, Simon Stylites would be forgotten
in half-an-hour. Was there ever before heard
of such a heroic case ? Did ever yet living
man have the prowess to propose to the girl
he loved ? It is an entirely new departure,
and should be noticed. It is quite unique."

" Don't be horrid," says his wife. " You know exactly what I mean—that it is a delightful ending to what promised to be a miserable muddle. And he *is* so charming —isn't he now, Freddy ? "

" *Is* he ? " asks Mr. Monkton, regarding her with a thoughtful eye.

" You can see for yourself. He is so *satisfactory*. I always said he was the very husband for Joyce. He is so kind, so earnest, so sweet in every way."

" *Nearly* as sweet as I am, eh ? " There is stern enquiry now in his regard.

" Pouf ! I know what *you* are of course. Who would, if I wouldn't ? But really, Freddy, *don't* you think he will make her an ideal husband ? So open, so frank ? So free from everything—everything—oh well, everything—*you* know."

" I don't," says Monkton uncompromisingly.

"Well—everything hateful—I mean. Oh ! she is a lucky girl ! "

" *Nearly* as lucky as her sister," says

Monkton, growing momentarily more stern in his determination to uphold his own cause.

"Don't be absurd! I declare," with a little burst of amusement, "when he—they —told me about it, I never felt so happy in my life."

"Except when you married *me*." He throws quite a tragical expression into his face, that is, however, lost upon her.

"Of course, with her present fortune she might have made what the world would call a more distinguished match. But his family is unexceptionable, and he has *some* money ; not much I know, but still, some. And even if he hadn't, she has now enough for both. After all," with noble disregard of the necessaries of life. "*What* is money?"

"Dross! mere dross!" says Mr. Monkton.

"And he is just the sort of man not to give a thought to it."

"He couldn't, my dear. Heroes of Romance are quite above all that sort of thing."

"Well, *he* is, certainly," says Mrs. Monkton, a little offended. "You may go on pretending as much as you like, Freddy, but I know you think about him just as I do. He is exactly the sort of charming character to make Joyce happy."

"Nearly as happy as I have made *you!*" says her husband severely.

"Dear me, Freddy, I really *do* wish you would try and forget yourself for one moment!"

"I *might* be able to do that, my dear, if I were quite sure that *you* were not forgetting me too!"

"Oh! as to *that!* I declare you are a perfect baby! You love teasing. Well—*there* then!" The "*there*" represents a kiss, and Mr. Monkton, having graciously accepted this tribute to his charms, condescends to come down from his mental elevation, and discuss the new engagement, with considerable affability. Once indeed, there is a dangerous lapse back into his old style, but this time there seems to be some occasion for it.

"When they stood there stammering and stuttering, Freddy, and looking so awfully silly, I declare I was so glad about it that I actually kissed him!"

"What?" says Mr. Monkton. "And you have lived to tell the tale? You have therefore lived too long. Perfidious woman, prepare for death!"

"I declare I think *you'd* have done it," says Barbara eloquently. Whereupon, having reconsidered her speech, they both give way to mirth.

"I'll try it when I see him," says Monkton. "Even a Hero of Romance couldn't object to a chaste salute from me."

"He is coming to dinner. I hope when you do see him, Freddy,"—anxiously this— "you will be very sober about it."

"Barbara! You know I *never* get—er— that is—not *before* dinner at all events."

"Well, but promise me now, you will

be very serious about it. They are taking it very seriously, and they won't like it if you persist in treating it as a jest."

" I'll be a perfect judge."

" I know what *that* means," indignantly. " That you are going to be as frivolous as possible."

" My *dear* girl ! If the Bench could only hear you. Well, there then ! Yes, *really !* I'll be everything of the most desirable. A regular funeral mute. And," seeing she is still offended, " I *am* glad about it, Barbara. Honestly pleased. I think him as good a fellow as I know, and Joyce another."

Having convinced her of his good faith in the matter, and agreed with her on every single point, and so far perjured himself as to remember perfectly and accurately the very day and hour on which, three months ago, she had said that she *knew* Joyce preferred Felix to Beauclerk, he is forgiven, and presently allowed to depart in peace with another " *There* " even warmer than the first.

But it is unquestionable that she keeps a severe eye on him all through dinner, and so forbids any trifling with the sacred topic. It would have put the poor things out so ! she has said to herself. And indeed it must be confessed that the lovers are very shy and uncomfortable, and that conversation drifts a good deal, and is only carried on regularly by fits and starts. But later, when Felix has unburdened his mind to Monkton during the quarter of an hour over their wine—when Barbara has been compelled in fear and trembling to leave Freddy to his own devices—things grow more genial, and the extreme happiness that dwells in the lovers' hearts is given full play. There is even a delightful half-hour granted them upon the balcony, Barbara having—like the good angel she is—declared that the night is almost warm enough for June.

CHAPTER XVIII.

"Great discontents there are, and many murmurs."

"There is a kind of mournful eloquence
In thy dumb grief."

LADY BALTIMORE too had been very pleased by the news, when Felix told her next morning of his good luck. In all her own great unhappiness she had still a kindly word and thought for her cousin and his *fiancée*.

"One of the *nicest* girls," she says, pressing his hands warmly. "I often think indeed *the* nicest girl I know. You are fortunate, Felix, but," very kindly, "she is fortunate too."

"Oh! no. The luck is all on my side," says he.

"It will be a blow to Norman," she says presently.

"I think not," with an irrepressible touch of scorn. "There is Miss Maliphant."

" You mean that he can ' decline ' upon
her.   Of course, I can quite understand that
you do not like him," says she with a quick
sigh.   " But believe me, any heart he has
was really given to Joyce.   Well ! he must
devote himself to ambition now."

" Miss Maliphant can help him to that."

" No   No.   That is all knocked on the
head.   It appears—this is in strict confidence, Felix—but it appears he asked her
to marry him last evening and she refused."

Felix turns to her as if to give utterance
to some vehement words, and then checks
himself.   After all, why add to her unhappiness ?   Why tell her of that cur's
baseness ?   Her own brother too !   It would
be but another grief to her.

To think he should have gone from *her*
to Miss Maliphant !   What a pitiful creature.
Beneath contempt.   Well ! if his pride sur-
vives those two downfalls, both in one day,
it must be made of leather.   It does Felix
good to think of how Miss Maliphant must

have worded *her* refusal! She is not famous for grace of speech. He must have had a real bad time of it. Of course Joyce had told him of her interview with the sturdy heiress.

" Ah ! she refused ? " says he, hardly knowing what to say.

" Yes. And not very graciously, I'm afraid. He gave me the mere fact of the refusal—no more—and only that because he had to give a reason for his abrupt departure. You know he is going this evening ? "

" No, I did not know it. Of course, under the circumstances——"

" Yes ; he could hardly stay here. Margaret came to me and said *she* would go, but I would not allow that. After all, every woman has a right to refuse or accept as she wills."

" True."

His heart gives an exultant leap as he remembers how *his* love had willed.

" I only wish she had not hurt him in

the refusal.   But I could see he was wounded.
He was not in his usual careless spirits.   He
struck me as being a little—well—you know
—a little——"

She hesitates.

"Out of temper?" suggests Felix, involuntarily.

"Well—*yes*.   Disappointment takes that
course with some people.   After all, it might
have been worse if he had set his heart on
Joyce and been refused."

"Much worse," said Felix, his eyes on the
ground.

"*She* would have been a severe loss."

"Severe, indeed."

By this time Felix is beginning to feel
like an advanced hypocrite.

"As for Margaret Maliphant, I am afraid
he was more concerned about the loss of her
bonds and scrips than of herself.   It is a
terrible world, Felix, when all is told," says
she, suddenly crossing her beautiful, long,
white hands over her knees and leaning

towards him. There is a touch of misery so sharp in her voice that he starts as he looks at her. It is a momentary fit of emotion, however, and passes before he dare comment on it. With a heart nigh to breaking she still retains her composure and talks calmly to Felix, and lets him talk to her as though the fact that she is soon to lose for ever the man who once had gained her heart—that fatal once that means for always—in spite of everything that has come and gone—is as little or nothing to her. Seeing her sitting there, strangely pale indeed, but so collected, it would be impossible to guess at the tempest of passion and grief and terror that reigns within her breast. Women are not so strong to endure as men, and therefore, in the world's storms suffer most.

"It is a lovely world," says he, smiling, thinking of Joyce; and then, remembering her sad lot, his smile fades. "One might make, perhaps, a bad world better," he says, stammering.

"Ah! Teach me how!" says she, with a melancholy glance.

"There is such a thing as forgiveness! *Forgive him!*" blurts he out in a frightened sort of way. He is horrified at himself—at his own temerity—a second later, and rises to his feet as if to meet the indignation he has certainly courted. But to his surprise no such indignation betrays itself.

"Is that your advice?" says she, still with the thin white hands clasped over the knee, and the earnest gaze on his. "Well, well, well!"

Her eyes droop. She seems to be thinking; and he, gazing at her, refrains from speech with his heart sad with pity. Presently she lifts her head and looks at him.

"There; go back to your love," she says, with a glance that thrills him. "Tell her from me that if you had the whole world to choose from, I should still elect *her* as your wife. I like her—I love her! There—*go!*"

She seems to grow all at once very tired. Are those tears that are rising in her eyes? She holds out to him her hand.

Felix, taking it, holds it closely for a moment, and presently, as if moved to do it, he stoops and presses a warm kiss upon it.

She is so unhappy, and so kind, and so true. God deliver her out of her sorrows!

CHAPTER XIX.

"I would that I were low laid in my grave."

SHE is still sitting silent, lost in thought after Felix's departure, when the door opens once again to admit her husband.

His hands are full of papers.

"Are you at liberty?" says he. "Have you a moment? These"—pointing to the papers—"want signing. Can you give your attention to them now?"

"What are they?" asks she, rising.

"Mere law papers. You need not look so terrified." His tone is bitter. "There are certain matters that must be arranged before my departure—matters that concern your welfare, and the boy's. Here," laying the papers upon the davenport and spreading them out, "you sign your name here."

"But"—recoiling—"what is it? What does it all mean?"

"It is not your death warrant, I assure you," says he, with a sneer. "Come, sign!" Seeing her still hesitate, he turns upon her savagely; who shall say what hidden storms of grief and regret lie within that burst of anger?

"Do you want your son to live and die a poor man?" says he. "And there is yourself to be considered too. Once I am out of your way, you will be able to begin life again with a light heart; and this"—tapping the papers heavily—"will enable you to do it. I make over to you and the boy everything—at least, as nearly everything as will enable me to live."

"It should be the other way," says she. "*Take* everything, and leave us enough on which to live."

"Why?" says he, facing round; something in her voice that resembles remorse striking him.

" *We* shall have each other," says she,
faintly.

"Having happily got rid of such useless
lumber as the father and husband ! Well,
you will be the happier so," rejoins he with
a laugh that hurts *him* more than it hurts
her, though she cannot know that. "Two
is company, you know, according to the good
old proverb, three, trumpery. You and he
will get on very well without me, no
doubt."

"It is your arrangement," says she.

"If that thought is a salve to your con-
science, pray think so," rejoins he. "It
isn't worth an argument. We are only
wasting time."

He hands her the pen. She takes it mechanically, but makes no use of it.

"You will at least tell me where you are
going ? " says she.

"Certainly I should if I only knew myself.
To America first, but that is a big direction,
and I am afraid the tenderest love-letter

would not reach me through it. When your friends ask you, say I have gone to the North Pole. It is as likely a destination as another."

"But not to *know!*" says she, lifting her dark eyes to his—dark eyes that seem to glow like fire in her white face, "that would be terrible. It is unfair ; you should think—think——"

Her voice grows husky and uncertain. She stops abruptly.

"Don't be uneasy about that," says he. "I shall take care that my death, when it occurs, is made known to you as soon as possible. Your mind shall be relieved on that score with as little delay as I can manage. The welcome news shall be conveyed to you by a swift messenger."

She flings the pen upon the writing-table and turns away.

"Insult me to the last, if you will," she says, "but consider your son. He loves you. He will desire news of you from time to time.

It is *impossible* that you can put him out of
your life as you have put me."

"It appears *you* can be unjust to the last,"
says he, flinging her own accusation back
at her. "Have I put you out of my
life?"

"Ah! was I ever in it?" says she. "But
—you will write?"

"No; not a line. Once for all, I break
with you. Should my death occur, you will
hear of it. And I have arranged so that now
and after that event you and the boy will
have your positions clearly defined. That
is all you can possibly require of me. Even
if you marry again, your jointure will be
secured to you."

"Baltimore!" exclaims she, turning upon
him passionately. She seems to struggle
with herself for words. "Has marriage
proved so sweet a thing," cries she presently,
"that I should care to try it again. There;
go! I shall sign none of these things."
She makes a disdainful gesture towards the

loose papers lying on the table, and moves angrily away.

" You have your son to consider."

" Your son will inherit the title and the property without those papers."

" There are complications, however, that, perhaps, you do not understand."

"Let them lie then. I shall sign nothing."

" In that case you will probably find yourself immersed in troubles of the meaner kinds after my departure. The child cannot inherit until after my death, and——"

" I don't care," sullenly. " Go, if you will. I refuse to benefit by it."

" What a stubborn woman you are," cries he, in great wrath. " You have for years declined to acknowledge me as your husband. You have, by your manner, almost *demanded* my absence from your side. Yet now, when I bring you the joyful news that in a short time you will actually be rid of me, you throw a thousand difficulties in my path. Is it that you desire to keep me near you

for the purposes of torture ? It is too late
for that. You have gone a trifle too far.
The hope you have so clearly expressed in
many ways, that time would take me out
of your path, is at last about to be fulfilled."

"I have had no such hope."

"No ? You can look me in the face and
say that ? Saintly lips never lie, do they ?
Well, I'm sick of this life, if you are not.
I have borne a good deal from you, as I
told you before. I'll bear no more. I give
in. Fate has been too strong for me."

"You have created your own Fate."

"*You* are my Fate ! You are inexorable.
There is no reason why I should stay."

Here the sound of running, childish, pat-
tering footsteps can be heard outside the
door, and a merry little shout of laughter.
The door is suddenly burst open in rather
unconventional style and Bertie rushes into
the apartment, a fox terrier at his heels.
The dog is evidently quite as up to the
game as the boy, and both race tempestu-

ously up the room and precipitate themselves against Lady Baltimore's skirts. Round and round her the chase continues, until the boy, bursting away from his mother, dashes towards his father, the terrier after him.

There isn't so much scope for talent in a pair of trousers as in a mass of dainty petticoats, and, presently Bertie, growing tired, flings himself down upon the ground and lets the dog tumble over him there. The joust is virtually at an end.

Lady Baltimore, who has stood immovable during the attack upon her, always with that cold, white, stricken look upon her face, now points to the beautiful child lying panting, laughing, playing with the dog, at his father's feet.

" *There* is a reason," says she, almost inaudibly.

Baltimore shakes his head.

" I have thought all that out. It is not enough," says he.

" Bertie," says his mother wildly, turning

to the child. "Do you know this—that your father is going to leave you?"

"Going?" says the boy vaguely, forgetting the dog for a moment, and glancing upwards. "Where?"

"Away. For ever."

"Where?" says the boy again. He rises to his feet now and looks anxiously at his father. Then he smiles and flings himself into his arms. "*Oh, no*," says he, in a little, soft, happy, *sure* sort of way.

"For ever! For ever!" repeats Isabel, in a curious monotone.

"Take me up," says the child, tugging at his father's arms. "What does mamma mean? Where are you going?"

"To America, to shoot bears," returns Baltimore, with an embarrassed laugh. How near to tears it is!

"Real *live* bears?"

"Yes."

"Take me with you," says the child, excitedly.

"And leave mamma ? "

" Oh, she'll come too," says Bertie confi-
dently. " She'll come where I go." Where
he would go—the child ; but would she go
where the father went ? Baltimore's brow
darkens.

" I am afraid it is out of the question,"
he says, putting Bertie back again upon the
carpet, where the fox-terrier is barking
furiously, and jumping up and down in a
frenzied fashion, as if desirous of devouring
the child's calves. " The bears might eat
you. When you are big, and strong——"

" You will come back for me ? " cries
Bertie, eagerly.

" Perhaps."

" He will not," breaks in Lady Baltimore
violently. " He will come back no more.
When he goes you will never see him again.
He has said so. He is going *for ever*."
These last two terrible words seem to have
sunk into her soul. She cannot cease from
repeating them.

" Let the boy alone," says Baltimore angrily.

The child is looking from one parent to the other. He seems puzzled, expectant, but scarcely unhappy. Childhood can grasp a great deal, but not all. The more unhappy the childhood the more it can understand of the sadder and larger ways of life. But children delicately brought up and clothed in love from the cradle, find it hard to realize that an end to their happiness can ever come.

" Tell me, papa," says he at last, in a vague, sweet little way.

" What is there to tell ? " replies his father, with a most meagre laugh, " except that I saw Beecher bringing in some fresh oranges half-an-hour ago. Perhaps he hasn't eaten them all yet, If you were to ask him for one——"

" I'll find him," cries Bertie brightly, forgetting everything but the present moment. " Come, Trixy, come," to his dog. " You shall have some too."

" You see there won't be much trouble with him," says Baltimore, when the boy has run out of the room in pursuit of oranges. " It will take him a day, perhaps, and after that—he will be quite your own. If you won't sign these papers to-day, you will, perhaps, to-morrow. I had better go and tell Hansard that you would like to have a little time to look them over."

He walks quietly down the room, opens the door, and closes it after him.

CHAPTER XX

" This is that happy morn,
    That day, long-wishéd day
Of all my life so dark,
(If cruel stars have not my ruin sworn,
    And fates my hopes betray),
    Which, purely white, deserves
An everlasting diamond should it mark."

HE has not, however, gone three yards down the corridor, when the door is again opened and Lady Baltimore's voice calls after him.

"*Baltimore!*" Her tone is sharp, high, agonized. The tone of one strung to the highest pitch of despair. It startles him. He turns to look at her. She is standing, framed in by the doorway, and one hand is grasping the woodwork with a hold so firm that the knuckles are shining white. With the other hand she beckons him to approach her. He obeys her. He is even so frightened at the strange, grey look in her face, that he draws her bodily into the room again, shutting the door with a pressure of the hand he can best spare.

" What is it ? " says he, looking down at her.

She has managed to so far overcome the faintness that has been threatening her, as to shake him off and stand free, leaning against a chair behind her.

" Don't go," says she hoarsely.

It is impossible to misunderstand her meaning. It has nothing whatever to do with his interview with the lawyer waiting so patiently down below, but with that wider wandering of his into regions unknown. She is as white as death.

" How is this, Isabel ? " asks he. He is as colourless as she is now. " Do you know what you are saying ? This is a moment of excitement—you do not comprehend what your words mean."

" Stay ! Stay for *his* sake ! "

" Is that all ? " says he, his eyes searching her.

"*For mine, then!*"

The words seem to scorch her. She covers her face with her hands and stands before him, stricken, dumb, miserable—confessed.

"For *yours!*"

He goes closer to her and ventures to take her hand. It is cold; cold as death. His is burning.

"You have given a reason for my staying, indeed," says he. "But what is the meaning of it?"

"*This*," cries she, throwing up her head, and showing him her shamed and grief-stricken face. "I am a coward! In spite of everything I would not have you go— *so far*."

"I see. I understand." He sighs heavily. "And yet that story was a foul lie. It is all that stands between us, Isabel—is it not so? But you will not believe."

There is a long silence, during which neither of them stir. They seem wrapped in thought, in silence, he still holding her hand.

" If it was a lie," says she at last, breaking the quiet round them by an effort. " *If* it was, would you so far forgive my distrust of you, as to be holding my hand like this ? "

" Yes. What is there I would not forgive you," says he. " And it *was* a lie ! "

" Cyril ! " cries she in great agitation, " take care ! It is a last moment ! Do you dare to tell me that still ? Supposing *your* story to be true, and mine—that woman's—false, how would it be between us then ? "

" As it was in the first good old time when we were married."

" You could forgive the wrong I have done you all these years ? Supposing——"

" Everything. All."

" *Ah !* " This sound seems crushed out of her. She steps backwards and a dry sob breaks from her.

"What is it?" asks he quickly.

"Oh, that I could, that I *dared* believe," says she.

"You would have proofs," says he coldly, resigning her hand. "My word is not enough. You *might* love me, did I prove worthy; your love otherwise is not strong enough to endure the pang of distrust. Was ever *real* love so poor a thing as that? However, you shall have them."

"What?" asks she, raising her head.

"The proofs you desire," responds he icily. "That woman—your friend—the immaculate one—died the day before yesterday. What? You never heard? And you and she——"

"She was nothing to me," says Lady Baltimore. "Nothing since——"

"The day she reviled me. And yet," with a most joyless laugh, "for the sake of a woman you cared so little about, that even now her death has not caused you a pang, you severed the tie that *should* have been the closest to you on earth. Well, she is dead; 'Heaven rest her soul,' as the peasants say. She wrote me a letter on her bed of death."

" Yes ?" eagerly.

" You still doubt," says he, with a stern glance at her. " So be it. You shall see the letter. Though how will that satisfy you ? You can always gratify your desire for suspicion by regarding it as a forgery. The woman herself is dead, so of course there is no one to contradict. *Do* think this all out," says he, with a contemptuous laugh, "before you commit yourself to a fresh belief in me. You see I give you every chance. To such a veritable ' Thomas ' in petticoats, every road should be laid open. Now," tauntingly, "will you wait here whilst I bring the proof ?"

He is gazing at her in a heart-broken sort of way. *Is* it the end ? Is it all really over ? There had been a faint flicker of the dying candle—a tiny glare

—and now—for all time is it to be dark-
ness ?

As for her ; ever since he had let her
hand go, she had stood with bent head
looking at it. He had taken it—he had
let it go. There seemed to be a promise
of Heaven—was it a false one ?

She is silent. And Baltimore, who had
hoped for one word of trust, of belief,
makes a gesture of despair.

" I will bring you the letter," he says,
moving towards the door.

When he *does* bring it, when she has
read it and satisfied herself of the loyalty
so long doubted, where, he asks himself,
will they two be then ? Farther apart than
ever ! He has forgiven a great deal—
much more than this—and yet, strange
human nature—he knows if he now leaves
the room and her presence, he will never
return to her again.

The letter she will see, but him—*never!*

The door is opened. He has almost

crossed the threshold. Once again her voice recalls him. Once again he looks back. She is holding out her arms to him.

"Cyril ! Cyril !" cries she, "I believe you."

She staggers towards him. Mercifully the fountain of her tears breaks loose ; she flings herself into his willing arms, and sobs out a whole world of grief upon his bosom.

It is a cruel moment, yet one fraught with joy as keen as the sorrow. A fire of anguish out of which both emerge purified, calmed, gladdened.

CHAPTER XXI.

"Lo, the winter is past, the rain is over and gone; the flowers appear on the earth; the time of the singing of birds has come."

THE vague suspicion of rain that had filled their thoughts at breakfast has proved idle. The sun is shining forth again with redoubled vigour as if laughing their silly doubts to scorn. Never was there so fair a day. One can almost *see* the plants growing in the garden, and from every bough the nesting birds are singing loud songs of joy.

The meadows are showing a lovely green, and in the glades and uplands the

> *" Daffodils*
> *That come before the swallow dares,"*

are uprearing their lovely heads. The air is full of sweet scents and sounds, and Joyce, jumping down from the drawing-room window that lies close to the ground, looks gladly round her. Perhaps it is not so much the beauty of the scene as the warmth of happiness in her own heart that brings the smile to her lips and eyes.

He will be here to-day. Involuntarily she raises one hand and looks at the ring that encircles her engaged finger. A charming ring —of pearls and sapphires. It evidently brings her happy thoughts, as, after gazing at it for a moment or two, she stoops and presses her lips eagerly to it. It is his first gift (though not his last), and therefore the most precious. *What* girl does not like receiving a present from her lover? The least mercenary woman on earth must feel a glow at her heart and a fonder recognition of her sweetheart's worth when he lays a love-offering at her feet.

Joyce, after her one act of devotion to *her* sweetheart, runs down the garden path, and towards the summer-house. She is not expecting Dysart until the day has well

grown into its afternoon ; but book in hand
she has escaped from all possible visitors to
spend a quiet hour in the old earwiggy
shanty at the end of the garden, sure of
finding herself safe there from interrup-
tions.

The sequel proves the futility of all
human belief.

Inside the summer-house, book in hand
likewise, sits Mr. Browne, a picture of
studious virtue.

Miss Kavanagh seeing him, stops dead
short, so great is her surprise, and Mr.
Browne, raising his eyes as if with a difficulty from the book on his knee, surveys
her with a calmly judicial eye.

"'Not here. Not here, my child,'"
quotes he, incorrectly. "You had better
try next door."

" Try for *what?* " demands she, indignantly.

" For *whom?* you mean."

" No, I don't," with increasing anger.

" Jocelyne," says Mr. Browne, severely,

" when one forsakes the path of truth it is only to tread in——"

" Nonsense," says Miss Kavanagh, irreverently.

" As you will ! " says he meekly. " But I assure you he is not here."

" I could have told *you* that," says she, colouring, however, very warmly. " I must say, Dicky, you are the most ingeniously stupid person I ever met in my life."

" To shine in even the smallest line in life is to achieve something," says Mr. Browne complacently. " And so you knew he wouldn't be here just now."

This is uttered in an insinuating tone. Miss Kavanagh feels she has made a false move. To give Dicky an inch is indeed to give him an ell.

" He ? Who ? " says she weakly.

" Don't descend to dissimulation, Jocelyne," advises he severely. " It is the surest road to ruin, if one is to believe the good old copy books. By he—you see *I* scorn

subterfuge—— I mean Dysart, the person
to whom in a mistaken moment you have
affianced yourself, as though—*I*—*I* were not
ready at any time to espouse you."

"*I'm* not going to be espoused," says
Miss Kavanagh, half laughing.

"No? I quite understood——"

"I won't have *that* word," petulantly.
"It sounds like something out of the dark
ages."

"So does he," says Mr. Browne.
"'*Felix*,' you know, so Latin. Quite like
one of the old monks. I shouldn't wonder
if he turned out a——"

"I wish you wouldn't teaze me, Dicky,"
says she. "You think you are amusing,
you know, but *I* think you are one of the
rudest people I ever met. I wish you
would let me alone."

"Ah, why didn't you leave *me* alone?"
says he with a sigh, that would have set a
furnace ablaze. "However," with a noble
determination to overcome his grief. "Let

the past lie. You want to go and meet Dysart, isn't that it ? And I'll go and meet him with you. Could self-sacrifice farther go ? 'Jim along Josy,' no doubt he is at the upper gate by this time flying on the wings of love ! "

"He is not," says Joyce, "and I wish once for all, Dicky, that you wouldn't call me 'Josy.' 'Jocelyne' is bad enough, but *Josy*. And I'm not going to 'Jim' anywhere, and certainly," with strong determination, "not with *you*." She looks at him with sudden curiosity. "What brought you here, to-day ?" asks she, most inhospitably it must be confessed.

"What brings me here every day. To see the unkindest girl in the world."

"She doesn't live here," says Miss Kavanagh. "Dicky," changing her tone suddenly, and looking at him with earnest eyes. "What is this I hear about Lady Baltimore and her husband ? Be sensible now, *do*, and tell me."

" They're going abroad together, with
Bertie. They've made it up," says he,
growing as sensible as even she can desire.
" It is such a complete make-up all round,
that they didn't even ask *me* to go with
them. However, I'm determined to join
them at Nice on their return from Egypt.
Too much billing and cooing is bad for
people."

" I'm so glad," says Joyce, her eyes fill-
ing with tears. " They are two such dear
people, and if it hadn't been for Lady——
By-the-bye, where *is* Lady Swansdown ? "

" Russia, I think."

" Well. I liked her too," says Joyce with
a sigh, " but she wasn't good for Baltimore,
was she ? "

" Not very," says Mr. Browne, drily. " I
should say on the whole that she disagreed
with him. Tonics are sometimes dangerous."

" I'm *so* delighted," says Joyce, still thinking of Lady Baltimore. " Well," smiling at

him, "why don't you go in and see Barbara ? "

"I *have* seen her—talked with her a long while, and bid her adieu. I was on my way back to the Court, having failed in my hope of seeing you, when I found this delightful nest of earwigs, and thought I'd stay and confabulate with them for a while in default of better companions."

"Poor Dicky ! " says she, "come with me, then, and I'll talk to you for half-an-hour."

"Too late," says he, looking at his watch. "There is only one thing left me now to say to you, and that is 'Good-bye' ! "

"Why this mad haste ? "

"Ah, ha ! *I* can have my little secrets, too," says he. "A whisper in your ear," leaning towards her.

"No, thank you," says she, waving him off with determination. "I remember your *last* whisper. There, if you can't stay, Dicky, good-bye, indeed. I'm going for a walk."

She turns away resolutely, leaving Mr. Browne to sink back upon the seat and continue his reading, or else to go and meet that secret he spoke of.

"I say," calls he, running after her, "you may as well see me as far as the gate, anyway."

It is evident the book, at least, has lost its charm. Miss Kavanagh, not being stony-hearted, so far gives in as to walk with him to a side gate, and, having finally bidden him adieu, goes back to the summer-house he has quitted, and opening *her* book, prepares to enjoy herself.

Vain preparation ! It is plain that the Fates are against her to-day. She is no sooner seated, with her book of poetry open on her knee, than a little flying form turns the corner, and Tommy precipitates himself upon her.

"What are you doing ?" asks he.

CHAPTER XXII.

"Lips are so like flowers,
   I might snatch at those,
Redder than the rose-leaves,
   Sweeter than the rose."

"Love is a great master."

"I am reading," she says. "Can't you see that?"

"Read to me, then," says Tommy, scrambling up on the bench beside her, and snuggling himself under her arm. "I love to hear people."

"Well, not this, at all events," says Miss Kavanagh, placing the dainty copy of "The Muses of Mayfair" she has been reading on the rustic table in front of her.

"Why not that one? What is it?" asks Tommy, staring at the book

"Nothing you would like—horrid stuff—only poetry."

" What's poetry ? "

" Oh ! Nonsense, Tommy ! You know very well what poetry is. Your hymns are poetry."

This, she considers, will put an end to all desire for the book in question. It is a clever and a skilful move, but it fails signally. There is silence for a moment whilst Tommy cogitates, and then——

" Are *those* hymns ? " demands he, pointing at the discarded volume.

" N-o—not exactly."

This is scarcely ingenuous, and Miss Kavanagh has the grace to blush a little. She is the further discomposed in that she becomes aware, presently, that Tommy sees through her perfectly.

" Well, *what* are they ? " asks he.

" Oh—er—well—just poetry, you know."

" I don't ! " says Tommy, flatly, who is nothing if not painfully truthful, " let me hear them."

He pauses here, and regards her with a searching eye.

" They "—with careful forethought—" they aren't *lessons*, are they ? "

"No, they are not lessons," says his aunt, laughing. " But you won't like them, for all that. If you are athirst for literature, get me one of your own books, and I will read ' Jack the Giant Killer ' to you."

" I'm *sick* of him," says Tommy, most ungratefully, that tremendous hero having filled up many an idle hour of his during his short lifetime. " No "—nestling closer to her— " go on with your *po'try* one."

" You would hate it. It is worse than Jack," says she.

" Let me hear it," says Tommy, persistently.

" Well," says Miss Kavanagh, with a sigh, "if you *will* have it, at least don't interrupt."

She has tried very hard to get rid of him ; but, having failed in so signal a fashion, she gives herself up, with an admirable resignation, to the inevitable.

"What would I do that for?" asks Tommy, rather indignant.

"I don't know, I'm sure. But I thought I'd warn you," says she, wisely precautious. "Now, sit down there," pointing to the seat beside her, "and when you feel you have had enough of it, say so at once."

"That would be interrupting," says Tommy the Conscientious.

"Well, I give you leave to interrupt *so far*," says Joyce, glad to leave him a loophole that may ensure his departure before Felix comes, "but no farther—mind that."

"Oh! I'm minding," says Tommy, impatiently. "Go on. Why don't you begin?"

Miss Kavanagh, taking up her book once more, opens it at random. All its contents are sweetmeats of the prettiest, so she is not driven to a choice. She commences to read in a firm soft voice.

> "The wind and the beam loved the rose
> And the rose loved one:
> For who recks the——"

"What's that?" says Tommy.

"What's *what*?"

"You aren't reading it right, are you?"

"Certainly I am—why?"

"I don't believe a beam of wood could love *anything!*" says Tommy—"It's too heavy!'

"It doesn't mean a beam of *wood*."

"Doesn't it?" staring up into her face, "what's it mean, then? 'The beam that is in thine own eye'?"

He is now examining "her own eye," with great interest. As usual, Tommy is strong in Bible lore.

"I have no beam in my eye, I hope," says Joyce, laughing, "and at all events, it doesn't mean that either, the poet who wrote this meant a *sun*beam."

"Well, why couldn't he *say* so?" says Tommy, gruffly.

"I really think you had better bring me one of your own books," says Joyce. "I told you this would——"

"No," obstinately. "I like this. It sounds

so nice and *smoothy.* Go on," says Tommy,
giving her a nudge.

Joyce, with a sigh, reopens the volume, and
gives herself up for lost. To argue with
Tommy is always to know fatigue and nothing
else.   One never gains anything by it.

" Well, do be quiet now, and listen," says
she, protesting faintly.

" I'm listening like *anything !* " says Tommy.
And indeed now, at last, it seems as if he were.

So silent does he grow, as his aunt reads
on, that you might have heard a mouse
squeak.   But for the low soft tones of Joyce
no smallest sound breaks the sweet silence
of the day.   Miss Kavanagh is beginning to
feel distinctly flattered. If one can captivate
the flitting fancies of a child by one's eloquent
rendering of charming verse, what may one
not aspire to ?   There must be something in
her style, if it can reduce a boy of seven to
such a state of ecstatic attention, considering
the subject is hardly such an one as would
suit his tender years.

But Tommy was always thoughtful beyond his age. A dear, clever little fellow. So appreciative ! Far, *far* beyond the average ! He——

The mild sweetness of the spring afternoon, and her own thoughts, are broken in upon at this instant by the "dear, clever little fellow."

" He has just got to your waist now," says he, with an air of wild, subdued excitement.

" He ! *Who ?* WHAT ? " shrieks Joyce, springing to her feet ; a long acquaintance with Tommy has taught her to dread the worst.

" Oh, *there !* Of course you've knocked him down, and I *did* want to see how high he would go. I was tickling his tail to make him hurry," says Tommy in an aggrieved tone. " I can't see him anywhere now," peering about on the ground at her feet.

" Oh ! *what* was it, Tommy ? *Do* speak !" cries Joyce in a frenzy of fear and disgust.

" 'Twas an earwig," says Tommy, lifting a

seraphic face to hers. " And such a *big* one ! He was racing up your dress most beautifully, and now you've upset him. Poor thing! I don't believe he'll *ever* find his way back to you again."

" I should hope not indeed," says Miss Kavanagh hastily.

" He began at the very end of your frock," goes on Tommy, still searching diligently on the ground as if to find the earwig, with a view to restoring it to its lost hunting-ground ; "and he wriggled up so *nicely*. I don't know *where* he is now," sorrowfully, "unless"— with a sudden brightening of his expressive face—"he is up your petticoats."

" Tommy ! what a horrid *bad* boy you are," cries poor Joyce wildly. She gives a frantic shake to the petticoats in question. " Find him *at once*, sir ! He *must* be somewhere down there. I sha'n't have an instant's peace until I know where he is."

" I can't see him anywhere," says Tommy ; " maybe you'll *feel* him presently, and then we'll know. He isn't on your leg *now*—is he ? "

" Oh ! *Don't*," cries Joyce, who looks as if she is going to cry. She gives herself another vigorous shake, and stands away from the spot where Tommy evidently thinks the noxious beast in question *may* be, with her petticoats held carefully up in both hands. " Oh ! Tommy, *darling! Do* find him. He *can't* be up my petticoats, can he ? "

" He can. There's *nothing* they can't do," says Tommy, who is plainly revelling in the storm he has raised. Her open fright is beer and skittles to him. " Why did you stir ? He was as good as gold until then ; and there wasn't anything to be afraid of. I was watching him. When he got to your *ear*, I'd have told you. I wouldn't like him to make you deaf—but I wanted to see if he *would* go to your ear. But you spoiled all my fun, and now—where is he now ? " asks Tommy, with an awful suggestion in his tone.

" In the grass, perhaps ! I don't feel him

anywhere," says Joyce miserably, looking round her everywhere, and even over her shoulder.

"Sometimes they stay quiet a long time, and then they *crawl!*" says Tommy, the most horrible anticipation in his tone.

"Really, Tommy," cries his aunt indig-nantly, "I do think you are the most abomin-able boy I ever met in my life. There, go away! I certainly sha'n't read another line to you—either now—or—*ever!*"

"What is the matter?" asks a voice at this moment, that sounds close to her elbow. She turns round with a start.

"It is you, Felix!" says she colouring warmly. "It—oh! it's nothing! Only Tommy. And he said I had an earwig on me. And I was—just a little unnerved, you know."

"And no wonder," says her lover with delightful sympathy. "I can't bear that sort of wild animal myself. Tommy, you ought to be ashamed of yourself. When you saw him, why didn't you rise up and slay the destroyer of your aunt's peace ? There ! run away into the hall. You will find on one of the tables a box of chocolate. I told Mabel it was there, perhaps she——"

Like an arrow from the bow Tommy departs.

" He has evidently his doubts of Mabel," says Joyce laughing rather nervously. She is still shy with Felix. " He doesn't trust her."

" No." He has seated himself, and now draws her down beside him. " You were reading ? " he says.

" Yes."

" To Tommy ? "

" Yes," laughing more naturally this time.

" Tommy is a more learned person than one would have supposed. Is *this* the sort of thing he likes ? " pointing to Nydia's exquisite song.

" I am afraid not. Though he would insist upon my reading it. The earwig was evidently a far more engrossing subject than either the wind or the rose."

" And yet——" He has his arm round her now and is reading the poem over her shoulder.

" *You* are my rose," says he softly. " And you, do you love but one ? "

She makes a little mute gesture that might signify anything or nothing to the uninitiated, but to him is instinct with a most happy meaning.

" Am I that one, darling ? "

She makes the same little, silent movement again, but this time she adds to it by casting a swift glance upwards at him, from under her lowered lids.

" Make me *sure* of it," entreats he, almost in a whisper. He leans over her, lower, lower still. With a little, tremulous laugh, she raises her soft palm to his cheek, and tries to press him from her; but he holds her fast.

" *Make* me sure ! " he says again. There is a last faint hesitation on her part, and then, their lips meet.

" I have doubted, always—always a *little*,

ever since that night down by the river," says
he. "But now——"

"Oh, no ! you must not doubt me again,"
says she with tears in her eyes.

THE END.

PRINTED BY
KELLY & CO., MIDDLE MILL, KINGSTON-ON-THAMES;
AND GATE STREET, LINCOLN'S INN FIELDS, W.C.

31, Southampton Street, Strand,
London, **W.C.**

F. V. WHITE & CO.'S

LIST OF

PUBLICATIONS.

NEW
NOVELS AT ALL CIRCULATING LIBRARIES.

THE PLUNGER.
By HAWLEY SMART, Author of "The Outsider," &c. 2 vols.

APRIL'S LADY.
By Mrs. HUNGERFORD, Author of "Molly Bawn," "Phyllis," &c. 3 vols.

A HOMBURG BEAUTY.
By Mrs. EDWARD KENNARD, Author of "A Crack County," &c. 3 Vols.

JACK'S SECRET.
By Mrs. LOVETT CAMERON, Author of "In a Grass Country," &c. 3 Vols.

CRISS CROSS LOVERS.
By the Honble. Mrs. H. W. CHETWYND, Author of "A March Violet," &c. 3 Vols.

BLIND FATE.
By Mrs. ALEXANDER, Author of " The Wooing O't," " By Woman's Wit," &c. 3 Vols.

BRAVE HEART AND TRUE.
By FLORENCE MARRYAT, Author of "My Sister the Actress," &c. 3 Vols.

BASIL AND ANNETTE.
By B. L. FARJEON, Author of "Toilers of Babylon," &c. 3 Vols.

MARGARET BYNG.
By F. C. PHILIPS and PERCY FENDALL, Authors of "A Daughter's Sacrifice," &c. 2 Vols.

THE NEW DUCHESS.
By Mrs. ALEXANDER FRASER, Author of "Daughters of Belgravia," "A Leader of Society," &c. 3 Vols. (2nd Edition.)

TWO MASTERS.
By B. M. CROKER, Author of "Proper Pride," " Pretty Miss Neville," &c. 3 Vols.

THE LOVE OF A LADY.
By ANNIE THOMAS (Mrs. PENDER CUDLIP), Author of "Allerton Towers," "Kate Valliant," &c. 3 Vols.

CASTE AND CREED.
By Mrs. FRANK PENNY. 2 Vols. 21s.

A WILLING EXILE.
By ANDRÉ RAFFALOVICH, Author of "It is Thyself," &c. 2 Vols. 12s.

F. V WHITE & Co.. 31, Southampton street, Strand.

THE WORKS OF JOHN STRANGE WINTER,

UNIFORM IN STYLE AND PRICE.

Each in Paper Covers, 1/-; Cloth, 1/6. At all Booksellers & Bookstalls.

HE WENT FOR A SOLDIER. (4th Edition.)

FERRERS COURT. (4th Edition.)

BUTTONS. (6th Edition).

A LITTLE FOOL. (8th Edition.)

MY POOR DICK.
(7th Edition.) Illustrated by MAURICE GREIFFENHAGEN.

BOOTLES' CHILDREN.
(8th Edition.) Illustrated by J. BERNARD PARTRIDGE.

"John Strange Winter is never more thoroughly at home than when delineating the characters of children, and everyone will be delighted with the dignified Madge and the quaint Pearl. The book is mainly occupied with the love affairs of Terry (the soldier servant who appears in many of the preceding books), but the children buzz in and out of its pages much as they would come in and out of a room in real life, pervading and brightening the house in which they dwell."—*Leices'er Daily Post.*

THE CONFESSIONS OF A PUBLISHER.

"The much discussed question of the relations between a publisher and his clients furnishes Mr. John Strange Winter with material for one of the brightest tales of the season. Abel Drinkwater's autobiography is written from a humorous point of view; yet here, as elsewhere, 'many a true word is spoken in jest,' and in the conversations of the publisher and his too ingenuous son facts come to light that are worthy of the attention of aspirants to literary fame."—*Morning Post.*

MIGNON'S HUSBAND. (11th Edition.)

"It is a capital love story, full of high spirits, and written in a dashing style that will charm the most melancholy of readers into hearty enjoyment of its fun."—*Scotsman.*

THAT IMP. (10th Edition.)

"Barrack life is abandoned for the nonce, and the author of 'Bootles' Baby' introduces readers to a country home replete with every comfort, and containing men and women whose acquaintanceship we can only regret can never blossom into friendship."—*Whitehall Review.*

"This charming little book is bright and breezy, and has the ring of supreme truth about it."—*Vanity Fair.*

MIGNON'S SECRET. (14th Edition.)

"In 'Mignon's Secret' Mr. Winter has supplied a continuation to the never-to-be-forgotten 'Bootles' Baby.' . . . The story is gracefully and touchingly told."—*John Bull.*

THE WORKS OF JOHN STRANGE WINTER—*(Continued)*.

ON MARCH.   (8th Edition.)

"This short story is characterised by Mr. Winter's customary truth in detail, humour, and pathos."—*Academy.*

"By publishing 'On March,' Mr. J. S. Winter has added another little gem to his well-known store of regimental sketches. The story is written with humour and a deal of feeling."—*Army and Navy Gazette.*

IN QUARTERS.   (9th Edition.)

"'In Quarters' is one of those rattling tales of soldiers' life which the public have learned to thoroughly appreciate."—*The Graphic.*

"The author of 'Bootles' Baby' gives us here another story of military life, which few have better described."—*British Quarterly Review.*

ARMY SOCIETY: Life in a Garrison Town.

Cloth, 6/-; also in Picture Boards, 2/-. (9th Edition.)

"This discursive story, dealing with life in a garrison town, is full of pleasant go' and movement which has distinguished 'Bootles' Baby,' 'Pluck,' or in fact a majority of some half-dozen novelettes which the author has submitted to the eyes of railway bookstall patronisers."—*Daily Telegraph.*

"The strength of the book lies in its sketches of life in a garrison town, which are undeniably clever. . . . It is pretty clear that Mr. Winter draws from life."—*St. James's Gazette.*

GARRISON GOSSIP, Gathered in Blankhampton.

(A Sequel to "ARMY SOCIETY.") Cloth, 2/6; also in Picture Boards, 2/-. (4th Edition.)

"'Garrison Gossip' may fairly rank with 'Cavalry Life,' and the various other books with which Mr. Winter has so agreeably beguiled our leisure hours."—*Saturday Review.*

"The novel fully maintains the reputation which its author has been fortunate enough to gain in a special line of his own."—*Graphic.*

A SIEGE BABY. Cloth, 2/6; Picture boards, 2/-. (3rd Edition.)

"The story which gives its title to this new sheaf of stories by the popular author of 'Bootles' Baby' is a very touching and pathetic one. . . . Amongst the other stories, the one entitled, 'Out of the Mists' is, perhaps, the best written, although the tale of true love it embodies comes to a most melancholy ending."—*County Gentlemen*

BEAUTIFUL JIM.   (6th Edition.)

Cloth gilt, 2/6; also Picture Boards, 2/-.

MRS. BOB.   (4th Edition.) Cloth gilt, 2/6.

F. V. WHITE & Co., 31, Southampton Street, Strand.

MRS. EDWARD KENNARD'S SPORTING NOVELS.

At all Booksellers and Bookstalls.

MATRON OR MAID? Cloth, 2s. 6d. (2nd Edition.)

LANDING A PRIZE. (4th Edition.)
Cloth, 2/6.

OUR FRIENDS IN THE HUNTING FIELD.
Cloth, 2/6.

A CRACK COUNTY. (5th Edition).
Cloth gilt, 2/6 ; also Picture Boards, 2/-.

THE GIRL IN THE BROWN HABIT.
Cloth gilt, 2/6 ;   Picture Boards, 2/-.   (6th Edition.)

" ' Nell Fitzgerald ' is an irreproachable heroine, full of gentle womanliness, and rich in all virtues that make her kind estimable. Mrs. Kennard's work is marked by high tone as well as vigorous narrative, and sportsmen, when searching for something new and beguiling for a wet day or spell of frost, can hardly light upon anything better than these fresh and picturesque hunting stories of Mrs. Kennard's."— *Daily Telegraph.*

KILLED IN THE OPEN.
Cloth gilt, 2/6 ; Picture Boards, 2/-. (7th Edition.)

"It is in truth a very good love story set in a framework of hounds and horses, but one that could be read with pleasure independently of any such attractions."— *Fortnightly Review.*
" ' Killed in the Open ' is a very superior sort of hunting novel indeed."—*Graphic.*

STRAIGHT AS A DIE.
Cloth gilt, 2/6 ; Picture Boards, 2/-. (7th Edition.)

"If you like sporting novels I can recommend to you Mrs. Kennard's 'Straight as a Die.'"—*Truth.*

A REAL GOOD THING.
Cloth gilt, 2/6.   Also Picture Boards, 2/-. (7th Edition.)

"There are some good country scenes and country spins in 'A Real Good Thing.' The hero, poor old Hopkins, is a strong character."—*Academy.*

TWILIGHT TALES. (*Illustrated.*) Cloth gilt, 2/6.

BY THE SAME AUTHOR.
In Paper Covers, 1/- ; Cloth, 1/6.

THE MYSTERY OF A WOMAN'S HEART.

A GLORIOUS GALLOP. (2nd Edition.)

F. V. WHITE & Co., 31, Southampton Street, Strand.

MRS. ALEXANDER'S NOVELS.

At all Booksellers and Bookstalls.

A FALSE SCENT.

Paper Covers, 1/-; Cloth, 1/6. (Third Edition.)

A LIFE INTEREST.

Cloth, 2/6. Also Picture Boards, 2/-. (Third Edition.)

BY WOMAN'S WIT.

(3rd Edition.)   Picture Boards, 2/-.

> " In Mrs. Alexander's tale
> Much art she clearly shows
> In keeping dark the mystery
> Until the story's close ! "—*Punch.*

MONA'S CHOICE.   Cloth, 2/6.

"Mrs. Alexander has written a novel quite worthy of her."—*Athenæum.*

". . . it is pleasant and unaffected."—*Saturday Review.*

"The story is pleasantly told, and some of the subsidiary characters are specially good. Mr. Craig, Mona's uncle, is indeed a triumph of truthful and humorous delineation, and we think that on the whole ' Mona's Choice ' must be considered Mrs. Alexander's best novel."—*Spectator.*

"RITA'S" NEW NOVELS.

Each in Paper Covers, 1/-; Cloth, 1/6. At all Booksellers and Bookstalls.

THE DOCTOR'S SECRET.   (2nd Edition.)

A VAGABOND LOVER.

THE MYSTERY OF A TURKISH BATH.

(2nd Edition.)

"Every fresh piece of work which ' Rita ' publishes, shows an increase of power, and a decided advance on the last. The booklet contains some very smart writing indeed."—*Whitehall Review.*

THE SEVENTH DREAM. A Romance.

" . . . is a powerful and interesting study in weird effects of fiction. It will hold the close attention of its readers from first to last, and keep them entertained with changing sensations of wonder."—*Scotsman.*

POPULAR WORKS

At all Booksellers and Bookstalls.

By WILLIAM DAY,

Author of " The Racehorse in Training," " Reminiscences of the Turf," &c.

TURF CELEBRITIES I HAVE KNOWN.

1 Vol., 16s.

At all Libraries and Booksellers.

By GUSTAV FREYTAG.

REMINISCENCES OF MY LIFE.

Translated from the German by KATHARINE CHETWYND.

In Two Vols., 18s.

By MRS. ARMSTRONG.

GOOD FORM.

(2nd Edition.)

A Book of Every Day Etiquette.

Limp Cloth, 2s.

By PERCY THORPE.

HISTORY OF JAPAN.

Cloth, 3s. 6d.

By PARNELL GREENE.

ON THE BANKS OF THE DEE.

A LEGEND OF CHESTER.

Cloth, 5s.

By W. GERARD.

BYRON RE-STUDIED IN HIS DRAMAS.

Cloth, 5s.

THE VISION, and other Poems.

Cloth, 3s. 6d.

F. V. WHITE & Co., 31, Southampton Street, Strand.

ONE VOLUME NOVELS

BY POPULAR AUTHORS.

Crown 8vo., Cloth, 2s. 6d. each.

AT ALL BOOKSELLERS AND BOOKSTALLS.

BY JOHN STRANGE WINTER.

MRS. BOB.
BEAUTIFUL JIM.
A SIEGE BABY.
GARRISON GOSSIP.

BY MRS. EDWARD KENNARD.

MATRON OR MAID?
LANDING A PRIZE.
A CRACK COUNTY.
OUR FRIENDS IN THE HUNTING-FIELD.
A REAL GOOD THING.
STRAIGHT AS A DIE.
THE GIRL IN THE BROWN HABIT.
KILLED IN THE OPEN.
TWILIGHT TALES. (*Illustrated*).

BY HAWLEY SMART.

LONG ODDS.
THE MASTER OF RATHKELLY.
THE OUTSIDER.

BY B. L. FARJEON.

THE MYSTERY OF M. FELIX.
A YOUNG GIRL'S LIFE.
TOILERS OF BABYLON.
THE DUCHESS OF ROSEMARY LANE.

By MAY CROMMELIN.

THE FREAKS OF LADY FORTUNE.

F. V. WHITE & Co., 31, Southampton Street, Strand.

ONE VOLUME NOVELS—(Continued).

BY F. C. PHILIPS & C. J. WILLS.

SYBIL ROSS'S MARRIAGE.

BY MRS. ALEXANDER.

A LIFE INTEREST.
MONA'S CHOICE.

BY MRS. LOVETT CAMERON.

A LOST WIFE.
THIS WICKED WORLD.
THE COST OF A LIE.

BY JUSTIN M'CARTHY, M.P., & MRS. CAMPBELL PRAED.

THE LADIES' GALLERY.
THE RIVAL PRINCESS.
MRS. ROBERT JOCELYN.
THE M.F.H.'S DAUGHTER.

BY BRET HARTE.

THE CRUSADE OF THE "EXCELSIOR."

BY THE HONBLE. MRS. FETHERSTONHAUGH.

DREAM FACES.

BY FERGUS HUME.

THE MAN WITH A SECRET.
MISS MEPHISTOPHELES.

BY MRS. HUNGERFORD, AUTHOR OF "MOLLY BAWN."

THE HONBLE. MRS. VEREKER.
A LIFE'S REMORSE.

BY "RITA."

SHEBA.
MISS KATE.

BY MRS. ALEXANDER FRASER.

DAUGHTERS OF BELGRAVIA.
SHE CAME BETWEEN.

BY MAY CROMMELIN & J. MORAY BROWN.

VIOLET VYVIAN, M.F.H.

BY F. C. PHILIPS & PERCY FENDALL.

A DAUGHTER'S SACRIFICE.

" POPULAR " NOVELS.

Picture Boards, 2s. each.

AT ALL BOOKSELLERS AND BOOKSTALLS.

———◆———

BEAUTIFUL JIM.   By JOHN STRANGE WINTER,
Author of " Bootles' Baby," &c.   (Sixth Edition.)

GARRISON GOSSIP.   By the same Author.
(Fourth Edition.)

A SIEGE BABY.   By the same Author.
(Third Edition.)

ARMY SOCIETY; Or, Life in a Garrison Town.
By the same Author.   (Ninth Edition.)

THE MASTER OF RATHKELLY. By HAWLEY
SMART.   (Fifth Edition.)

THE OUTSIDER. By HAWLEY SMART. (Sixth
Edition.)

A LIFE INTEREST.   By Mrs. ALEXANDER,
Author of " The Wooing O't," &c.   (Third
Edition.)

THE GIRL IN THE BROWN HABIT. By Mrs.
EDWARD KENNARD, Author of " A Real Good
Thing," " A Crack County," &c. (Sixth Edition.)

A REAL GOOD THING.   By the same
Author.   (Seventh Edition.)

KILLED IN THE OPEN. By the same Author. (Seventh Edition.)

STRAIGHT AS A DIE. By the same Author. (Seventh Edition.)

A CRACK COUNTY. By the same Author. (Fifth Edition.)

THIS WICKED WORLD. By Mrs. LOVETT CAMERON. (Fourth Edition.)

A DEVOUT LOVER. By the same Author. (Third Edition.)

THE COST OF A LIE. By the same Author. (Second Edition.)

A DEAD PAST. By the same Author.

A NORTH COUNTRY MAID. By the same Author.

THE CRUSADE OF THE "EXCELSIOR." By BRET HARTE, Author of "Devil's Ford," &c.

THE HONBLE. MRS. VEREKER. By Mrs. HUNGERFORD, Author of "Molly Bawn," "A Life's Remorse," &c.

MISS MEPHISTOPHELES. By FERGUS HUME, Author of "The Mystery of a Hansom Cab," "The Piccadilly Puzzle," &c. A New and Original Novel. (Fourth Edition.)

A WOMAN'S FACE. By FLORENCE WARDEN, Author of "The House on the Marsh," &c.

ONE SHILLING NOVELS.

In Paper Covers; Cloth, 1s. 6d.

At all Booksellers and Bookstalls.

HE WENT FOR A SOLDIER. By JOHN STRANGE WINTER, Author of "Bootles' Baby," &c. (4th Edition.)

FERRERS COURT. By the same Author. (4th Edition.)

BUTTONS. By the same Author. (6th Edition).

A LITTLE FOOL. By the same Author. (8th Edition.)

THE PICCADILLY PUZZLE. By FERGUS HUME, Author of "The Mystery of a Hansom Cab," &c.

THE GENTLEMAN WHO VANISHED. By the same Author.

MY WONDERFUL WIFE! A Study in Smoke. By MARIE CORELLI, Author of "A Romance of Two Worlds," &c. (2nd Edition.)

A TROUBLESOME GIRL. By Mrs. HUNGERFORD, Author of "Molly Bawn," &c. (5th Edition.)

HER LAST THROW. By the same Author.

A STRANGE ENCHANTMENT. By B. L. FARJEON, Author of "Devlin the Barber," &c.

A VERY YOUNG COUPLE. By the same Author.

THE PERIL OF RICHARD PARDON. By the same Author. (2nd Edition.)

A FRENCH MARRIAGE. By F. C. PHILIPS, Author of "As in a Looking Glass," &c.

A VAGABOND LOVER. By "RITA," Author of "The Mystery of a Turkish Bath," &c.

THE LAST COUP. (3rd Edition.) By HAWLEY SMART, Author of "Cleverly Won," &c.

A BLACK BUSINESS. By the same Author. (3rd Edition.)

A FALSE SCENT. (3rd Edition.) By Mrs. ALEXANDER.

ONE SHILLING NOVELS—*(Continued)*.

MY POOR DICK. (7th Edition.) By JOHN STRANGE WINTER. (With Illustrations by MAURICE GREIFFENHAGEN.)

BOOTLES' CHILDREN. (8th Edition.) By JOHN STRANGE WINTER. (With Illustrations by J. BERNARD PARTRIDGE.)

THE CONFESSIONS OF A PUBLISHER. By the same Author.

MIGNON'S HUSBAND. (11th Edition.) By the same Author.

THAT IMP. (10th Edition.) By the same Author.

MIGNON'S SECRET. (14th Edition.) By the same Author.

ON MARCH. (8th Edition.) By the same Author.

IN QUARTERS. (9th Edition.) By the same Author.

A GLORIOUS GALLOP. (2nd Edition.) By Mrs. EDWARD KENNARD.

THE MYSTERY OF A WOMAN'S HEART. By the same Author.

THE MYSTERY OF A TURKISH BATH. (2nd Edition.) By "RITA."

THE DOCTOR'S SECRET. By the same Author. (2nd Edition.)

THE SEVENTH DREAM. A Romance. By the same Author.

DEVIL'S FORD. By BRET HARTE.

TOM'S WIFE. By Lady MARGARET MAJENDIE, Author of "Fascination," &c.

IN A GRASS COUNTRY. By Mrs. LOVETT CAMERON. (9th Edition.)

THE CONFESSIONS OF A DOOR MAT. By ALFRED C. CALMOUR, Author of "The Amber Heart," &c.

CITY AND SUBURBAN. By FLORENCE WARDEN, Author of "The House on the Marsh," &c. (2nd Edition.)

MY SISTER THE ACTRESS. By FLORENCE MARRYAT.

www.ingramcontent.com/pod-product-compliance
Lightning Source LLC
Chambersburg PA
CBHW021057030726
47496CB00006B/1875